# PERFECT STRANGERS

**Perfect Strangers: Bad Bear Down**

Copyright © 2023 by Lloyd F. Stamy, Jr.

All rights reserved. No part of this book may be used or reproduced in any manner whatsoever without written permission of the author.

This book is a work of fiction. Excepting those where prior permission has been obtained, the names, characters, places, and incidents are the product of the author's imagination or are used fictitiously. Any resemblance to actual events, locales, or persons, living or dead, is coincidental.

*Author photo on back cover courtesy of* Rick Walker

ISBN 979-8-9884351-2-9
Library of Congress Control Number: 2023942149

*Published by*

# PERFECT STRANGERS

BAD BEAR DOWN

LLOYD STAMY

# CONTENTS

# FOREWORD

FIRST, AN ADMISSION. One might assume that penning a second sequel, or follow-on third novel, would be easy, but it isn't, or at least wasn't for me. The obstacle was not the writing itself, which is always a thoroughly enjoyable experience and routine daily pastime – even if only for my own amusement. Rather, the difficulty was trying to incorporate the important connections to what had been written previously. Reintroducing the characters in ways that would provide the reader sufficient insight and background, but without having to repeat the entire backstory of their lives, was challenging.

Hopefully, I have conveyed enough context and provided ample throwback references for those of you who haven't yet read the two preceding books, while not boring those who have. Nevertheless, to do the characters justice, I encourage you to read both *Reunion of Strangers* and *Strangers No More* beforehand in order to fully grasp the historical framework and embrace the full essence of their personalities. Doing so will enhance your enjoyment, and you can trust me on this one.

No doubt you will find a strong hint of resolution and overall conclusiveness to the story. However, whether carelessly or by intention, the door is left slightly ajar for fleshing out yet another sequel in the series, though for the reason first mentioned above, I make no such promise. As for the future, my plan is to keep writing *something* every day until inevitably drifting further into curmudgeonhood.

I am grateful for the encouragement of my beloved friends and readers for their inspiration to continue the *Hap Franklin*

*Series*, and salute my wife, Mary Margaret, for her abiding patience with me while doing so. Lastly, as with all previous works, any proceeds (author commissions and royalties) earned from the publication of this book will be donated to charity.

—LLOYD F. STAMY, JR., *May, 2023*

# PREAMBLE

STILL SEETHING AFTER YEARS OF MOURNING, former CIA operative Hap Franklin emerges from retirement to avenge the Kremlin-ordered murder of his wife. The Russian president's waning popularity in the wake of worldwide condemnation over his launching an unprovoked war, coupled with its devastating effects on an already flagging domestic economy, present Hap with a perfect opportunity to bring down the Bad Bear. However, failing to resist a variety of temptations in his path complicate and elevate Hap's quest to a near existential journey.

Beyond the intrigue of such a daunting mission is the much anticipated progression of the epic tale already familiar to seasoned readers. The overarching thread that binds the three-book series together is the abiding lifelong kinship of two childhood friends by a liaison forged in the seventh grade. Inextricably bound to each other from the start and fated from its inception, their entanglement is complex, complicated, conflicted, and often confusing, but always joyful. In *Perfect Strangers – Bad Bear Down*, the durability of that longstanding relationship is put to a final test.

His noble ambitions aside, Hap remains tragically flawed in the usual ways that befall most heroes, including spiritual anxiety and guilt over misdeeds such as the taking of another's life and the partaking of fruit that may have been forbidden, but not necessarily prohibited. As with all characters of any complexity, navigating the strong undercurrent of life's enticements is a universal endeavor. Consequently, the primary storyline is often overshadowed by Hap's ongoing emotional struggle with his faith for both guidance and forgiveness in order to get life right while there is still time. Such a pilgrimage was supposed to absolve all trespasses, soothe his troubled soul, and restore life's happiness… but perhaps that would prove to be another of Hap's mistaken expectations.

# THE STARTING GATE

MARY HAD BEEN HER NAME WHEN CHRISTENED, but after being called Marsidotes by her overly adoring parents for far too long, her friends in junior high began calling her by a different nickname. Initially she disliked the new handle as well, but its origin was her own fault. In those days all girls who weren't blonde wanted to be. Some, especially the brunettes, squeezed lemons on their hair and sat in the sun to make the transition. Others, like Mary, used a reflector at the same time to deepen their tans.

The combination of lightening her hair and constant sunbathing earned Mary a brand new name – Sunny…Sunny Day. Sure, it was corny, and everyone else knew that but Sunny. But she liked the sound of it even though it conjured up images of everything under the sun – from a tanning salon to a nursing home. Even worse, her father thought it sounded like a porn star. The name stuck, and after reaching the age of majority, she further disappointed her parents by making the change a legally permanent one.

Given Sunny's Nordic ancestry, her family's surname of Day must have been shortened from something longer, and perhaps more fearsome sounding, to reflect the Germanic farmers and part-time warriors who settled in Scandinavia before becoming raiders of the North Sea. Because of the complexity of her inescapable DNA soup, it wasn't surprising that Sunny didn't take direction or criticism well. Instead, she quickly dismissed any objections to her strong-willed, if not dominating nature by believing it was just the Viking in her.

Once out of the starting gate there was no stopping the self-styled Sunny Day. Despite her rebellious nature, she was a gifted student and excelled in all disciplines – in fact, so much so that Stanford awarded her a full-boat scholarship. Beyond the economic windfall, her proud parents were overjoyed, but later infuriated when she chose to major in Slavic Languages and Literature. Though convinced Sunny was wasting her time and throwing her life away, they were powerless to persuade her otherwise. They might have tolerated her majoring in the Romance languages instead, where Sunny already had a leg up. Having spent her junior year abroad in France as a foreign exchange student, Sunny was not only conversant in French, but also could speak enough Italian to get by.

Like many of the same vintage, and long before Sunny was born, her parents had witnessed a defiant Nikita Khrushchev beat his shoe on the table at the United Nations in 1960. They also remembered his chilling "We will bury you" quote when taunting America, which was all they ever wanted to know about the USSR. Given that background, their ongoing disapproval was expected. As for Sunny, she figured knowing something about the enemy might come in handy if America lost the Cold War. Oddly enough, her unusual choice of major would eventually prove to be a life saver down the road after the Soviets became just plain old Russians.

By her third year, Sunny was so immersed in the language that Russian could be mistaken for her native tongue. Guttural, harsh, and angry to the ear, it was an odd-sounding language to the listener, but proved easier to speak than she had expected. The Cyrillic, or Russian alphabet, had 33 letters and was based on Greek language, whereas the English alphabet had 26 letters and originated from Latin. It wasn't unusual for Sunny not only to think, but sometimes even dream in her newly adopted language. She was equally comfortable using a Russian keyboard, and could type 50 words per minute. Her manual dexterity wasn't exclusively limited to the mastery of a Cyrillic typewriter, though there were only a very select few on the Stanford campus who knew about that.

Her accomplishment in Slavic Languages and Literature didn't go unnoticed by the department's chair, who recognized that she was without peer among the students he'd encountered over the course of his tenure. Like others in his position at major universities across the country, he was on the lookout for exceptional students who had a keen interest in all things Russian. His role was to report top students of Sunny's caliber by contacting someone he had been led to believe was a State Department employee, but wasn't.

Decades before, it had been the CIA that put out such feelers to the few remaining schools that could afford to staff fields of interest related to Russia. Of course, as with most things in life, there was an expectation of the obligatory quid pro quo. To encourage ongoing referrals of students with the needed aptitude, top universities were awarded federal grants designated to make sure their Slavic programs weren't subject to an otherwise sharp budget knife due to scant enrollment. The federal pork became a routine perk, and the folks at Stanford were only too eager to return the favor. In Sunny Day's case, it meant her name was now on a secret shortlist at Langley for further vetting, clandestine observation, and possible recruitment.

All the while, Sunny's loving parents refused to give up on her. Their presumption was that she would return home from the Left Coast once she got over what they were convinced was a misguided stage in her life. But once again, they would be disappointed, as Sunny insisted on remaining in the Bay Area after graduation. She liked the location for many reasons beyond the temperate climate. Unlike most of California, San Francisco enjoyed some seasonality, but the overriding appeal for Sunny

was that the sophisticated Bay women looked eastward for fash-
ion-savvy guidance, and were always better dressed than the
glittery L.A. crowd.

To follow her artistic dream of becoming a painter, Sunny
needed support, and plenty of it. Always the renegade, it was not
her nature to seek help from her family, even though they hadn't
had to shell out a nickel for her education. As when meeting
any challenge, it didn't take long for her inner Viking to prevail.
Unwilling to become somebody's kept woman or just anybody's
wife, Sunny soon found success in selling high-end homes in
only the upscale neighborhoods of San Francisco. Part-time work
as an astute realtor was rewarding beyond her expectations, and
enabled her ongoing pursuit of remaining viscerally connected to
her art.

Never attending art school, Sunny came by her gift naturally.
Even as a youngster she noodled and doodled her way through
otherwise boring books by adding creative illustrations. Eventually such child's play evolved into much more serious artwork
and she was hooked for good. For Sunny, it was easy; she knew
what she liked and her clients liked what they saw. It was the
same way with her second career in real estate.

Though more at home when in her comfortable painter's
smock, she had a bedazzling wardrobe of fashionable ensembles
with an accompanying array of pumps in all flavors to match
every outfit. For Sunny, it was no different than pairing the
right pigments from her palette to fashion a masterpiece. In her
business, creating a little magic and allure was one of the keys to
earning big-ticket commissions on multimillion-dollar proper-
ties without much negotiation. As a result, everything in which
she adorned herself was fashionably tailored and snug-fitting
to showcase her model-like body and provide all onlookers a
stunning visual display of raw sensuality. She also had enough

self-awareness to recognize such preening as yet another dimension of her longing to be desired, but not necessarily loved.

Sunny was all business both day and night which, beyond her work, attracted the watchful eye of a recruiter for a federal agency charged with keeping the country free from foreign meddling. She had been in the agency's cross hairs since being targeted when at Stanford. As expected, recruiting Sunny proved to be a hard sell. Her reluctance to abandon a lucrative career in residential real estate for another part-time, but lower-paying gig as a spy, was typical. To further convince her of the opportunity, Bud Smith himself was summoned to help close the deal. As the CIA's Deputy Director for Operations, or DDO, it wasn't customary to enlist Bud's help in the recruitment of new hires, but recognizing Sunny's potential value to the dark side, he was willing to invest a day or two on the West Coast to secure a new asset. Having seen her file and the surveillance photos, he also wouldn't mind getting away from Langley to wine and dine such a fascinating and extraordinary woman on the agency's dime.

Bud was known for baiting the hook better than anyone. When hard pressed, he wasn't beyond draping himself in the American flag and pleading with, if not shaming, folks into embracing their patriotic duty. With Sunny it hadn't taken long, as Bud was convincing. Like he had with Hap Franklin before, Bud sealed the deal and Sunny became an official, yet anonymous, undercover federal employee. Because her first stop was Camp Peary, that temporary relocation back East put her in touch with family and old friends, but given the nature of her new job, that proved to be short-lived.

Sunny had it all going on, and it all worked for her. She also made use of it all when assigned to a senior agent for personal instruction. Once their training in tradecraft at The Farm was complete, new operatives were apprenticed to seasoned ones, and her mentor was one of the most celebrated. Bud had seen to that by the deliberate choice of his best veteran spook as her professor in the dark arts. It wasn't long before she too began worshipping her tutor. It was easy to warm up to a guy like Hap Franklin because he made their otherwise serious work fun. Sunny liked working with and under him, eventually in ways they could not avoid.

From the start, Hap knew that the spell she cast spelled trouble. There were some things in life you couldn't run away from fast enough. In time, Sunny would prove to be one of them. Try as he had to disguise if not suppress his feelings, Hap suspected she was well aware of his longings and ready to reciprocate them in kind. When first introduced by Bud, both had felt the same sense of urgency. Hap was immediately drawn to her full lips that formed the type of kissable mouth that all men dreamed about. Her pale blue eyes were piercing, sultry, and dreamy all at the same time. Sunny had all the makings of a good spy; her mind was brilliant and her instincts keen. Beyond those initial impressions, it wasn't long before Hap discovered so much more about her to covet. So far, his conduct as an operative had been exemplary and irreproachable, but exercising professional restraint when it came to Sunny turned out to be a tall order.

If forced to define Sunny in one word, most men would agree on *hot*, but that didn't capture the entire essence. She was so much more. *Captivating* would have been the word Hap might choose, with *complicated* a close second. Over the many years that had now passed since he last saw her, Hap remembered her with fondness tinged with lust. Jeans, a tight tee shirt, windblown hair and an ever present winsome smile suited her for nearly all occasions. She needed nothing beyond a single strand of pearls or simple gold necklace for adornment when dressing up. Sometimes that's all she wore, which was the way Hap usually thought about Sunny Day.

Sunny was the kind of woman who could break men's hearts, and she had. For the most part, she had been discriminating when choosing who would share her pillow. Much like painting, when she chose precisely from among a plethora of pigments before selecting the perfect hue, her choice of partners had been an equally artistic endeavor. There were other times when it wasn't, but such men were chosen just as deliberately…and by intention. Those occasions were nothing beyond overnighters when needed in desperation to feed the carnal beast that raged within her. Once gratified, she quickly moved on, and those odd bedfellows were summarily dismissed and discarded – most by sunrise.

Her finished artwork was like that as well. She knew not to fall in love with her pieces, as they would soon be hanging in the homes of perfect strangers and never to be seen again. The short-lived relationship with Hap had been far different. Even after the passage of time should have erased it, the canvas of their passion remained unfinished. In those days he was married, and had made it clear from the start that she could never be anything beyond a colleague and certainly not an occasional paramour. That agreement worked for a time, but hadn't stopped Hap from thinking about Sunny Day in ways he shouldn't have.

# A SIREN'S CALL

THOUGH TWENTY YEARS HAD PASSED since the indiscretion, Hap's memory of it remained vivid. It should never have happened, but it had, and that was that. It was one of those things that couldn't be undone or permanently erased. He had replayed it hundreds of times in his mind's eye. Why? Because though troublesome, it was a fond memory. The encounter with Sunny in Switzerland needed no further embellishment. Besides, any exaggeration would only serve to diminish its authenticity. But neither could his role in their brief affair be downplayed; it was just wrong.

It was their first and only clandestine mission together. They had been paired for it by Bud Smith himself – not only because Hap and Sunny had the right combination of skill sets for the job, but Bud was also curious if they could behave themselves when on assignment. The target was a Russian double agent and expert skier known only as Boris by his CIA handler. Boris had committed the cardinal sin of double crossing Langley, which was an unforgivable mistake in the spy business. The plan was to take him out when most vulnerable, which was while skiing in either Zermatt or Saint Moritz. Every year Boris spent a week in both places, taking the Glacier Express train between the two. Bud's contingency plan was to make the hit aboard the train, but that would be more problematic and messier than necessary. The least complicated way was to make it appear that Boris had a tragic accident on the slopes, and one that would claim his life.

Beyond his own prurient interest in whether Hap and Sunny might hook up, Bud had hand-picked them for a host of legitimate reasons. Beyond being accomplished skiers, they were methodical, calculating, careful, and lethal assassins. Acting in concert while masquerading as a couple lost on the mountain, it wouldn't be difficult to take Boris down and hide his body in an off-trail snow bank. They would bury Boris deep in the snowpack so no animals would find his carcass until the spring thaw. After coming close to extinction due to overhunting, bears and wolves had made a dramatic comeback and now thrived in the alpine forests. Once these ravenous predators discovered and had feasted on the well-preserved carrion, there would be nothing beyond Boris's scattered bones for identification.

Bud's advance team at Langley always took care of their agents' itineraries well in advance, including hotel reservations. Such planning would make the trip by Hap and Sunny appear more like a long-awaited vacation instead of its real intention – a quick hit followed by an even faster departure. The Suvretta House was chosen because that's where the better-heeled of the international jet set stayed when in Saint Moritz. The resort had a few private chalets for discreet visits by celebrities and royals, but Bud had considered that too risky for the couple he was putting in the field. Plus he wasn't about to foot the bill for such posh digs where some extracurricular hanky panky might occur. Instead, he decided that lodging the two in the main hotel was more than suitable. Bud had arranged for separate, but connecting, rooms, despite knowing that even this choice of accommodation might prove to be an enticement all by itself.

The flight from Gatwick to Zurich was uneventful, as they sat apart for security reasons. There was no such prohibition on the train from Zurich to Saint Moritz, so Hap and Sunny were able to enjoy the breathtaking Alps together from a private compartment. One of the Suvretta House drivers met them at the station in a Mercedes-Maybach S600 for the short mid-afternoon ride to the hotel. After checking in and surrendering their false passports, Hap and Sunny agreed to meet for a late dinner so they could shake off the jet lag by taking a nap beforehand. Neither of them slept well, and it was not because of the grim mission ahead of them over the next few days. Rather, their agitation was more about the excitement of their beds being separated by only a single wall. Both knew it could prove to be the gateway to an opportunity neither of them could resist.

When she entered the elegant dining room, Hap was already awaiting her arrival at the table nursing a dry vodka martini while privately fantasizing about how the evening might end. Sunny Day knew how to make an entrance, and that time was no different. To ensure that all eyes were riveted on her alone, Sunny hadn't dressed as she had been instructed, which was to blend in with the other ski bunnies. She wanted to stand out in a big way, and all for Hap's benefit. In lieu of the designer stretch pants, cashmere sweaters and fancy après ski boots worn by most of the other women diners, Sunny had chosen a tight skirt with high heels, which accentuated the calves of her shapely legs. She drew far more than a look by both the hungry men and jealous women already seated. The low-cut silk blouse would have been fetching enough all by itself, and had been chosen to enhance, if not punctuate, the ensemble…and no doubt to further feed what she hoped was Hap's growing arousal.

Even without meeting his stare, she could feel Hap's gaze, which went far beyond his usual furtive glance. This time she knew his eyes were running the full length of her body and taking it all in. Commanding such attention made her feel glamorous in ways far beyond what any others had ever accomplished. Almost from the beginning she had known Hap was like that, but for fear of being too suggestive, Sunny had always been able to dial it back. Tonight would be different. A full-throttled approach, bolstered by a brimming reservoir of self-confidence, was her battleplan.

Despite the attention she drew from the other diners, their evening together proved to be memorable due to the cuisine and leisurely pace they took while enjoying each course. Because it was the very first time they had been alone and safe from scrutiny, they took the time to get to know each other. Very little was held back about their personal lives – especially the dreams, triumphs, failures, and regrets that had brought them to this place and the kind of jobs they were charged to perform for Uncle Sam.

So engaging was Sunny that Hap didn't want it to end, but knew it must, as they had important work to do the next day and needed to be alert and well rested. Playing the roles that Bud had fashioned for them, they walked back to their rooms hand in hand, appearing like any other couple in love and on holiday. Once at her doorway, Hap thanked her for the wonderful evening and gave her a quick kiss on the cheek.

"Good night, Hap, but before you go, let's be clear about one thing."

"What's that, Sunny?"

"Well…just so you know, sex is usually as far as I'm willing to go on the first date."

With a dumbstruck Hap staring back at her in amazement, she just smiled and allowed the door to slowly close in his face. Had he misread the tea leaves? No, the lure was unmistakable. A variety of hooks had been well-baited and set, but he was not yet ready to be snagged. Besides, horseplay between agents was a big no-no, especially when on assignment. Bud would go ballistic if he ever found out, and somehow he had always managed to do so when others had violated the rules.

Once back in his room next door, Hap put on his pajamas and, after propping himself up in bed using only half the far-too-many pillows he found there, began reading one of the countless glossy tourist magazines spread about the suite in designer-like fashion. So far he had conquered the primal urges, but feared they might yet take over. Before turning out the light, he thought he overheard something coming from the next room. After hearing the distinctive sound of a thumb bolt turning open, he knew it was from Sunny's side of the adjoining doors. It was a siren call, and one he knew was irresistible.

# CROSSING THE LINE

ONFLICTED AS HE WAS, Hap could no longer avoid what he knew awaited him through the now unbolted door that connected their rooms. He considered removing his pajamas, but in case he was mistaken about her intentions, left them on. Besides, he thought it best not to startle her with what refused to be concealed. After knocking three times, he heard the faint but reassuring reply he expected.

"It's about time, Hap. What on earth have you been waiting for?"

"You know me, I was hoping for something a little more formal, like an engraved invitation slipped under the door."

He opened the unlatched door and, despite the darkness, was drawn straight to the foot of her bed and began disrobing. She switched on the bedside reading light to get a better look at him. Finding everything in working order as she had imagined it would be, Sunny smiled and beckoned him onward.

"Hap, I was beginning to think you were afraid of going too far."

"As T.S. Eliot once said, 'Only those who will risk going too far can possibly find out how far one can go.'"

"Well then, if you're done showing off your obvious readiness, you could start by crawling in bed so I can show you just how far that can be. By the way, I hope you have a carry permit for that."

"I've never considered it a lethal weapon."

"Well, if it were, it's obviously not concealed and certainly not standard issue."

Hap slid under the covers and found immediate comfort in the warm nakedness of her embrace. The mouth he had longed to kiss and taste exceeded his expectations, as did all other parts of her lithe body once he made his way there. The prelude included pausing to nestle in her cleavage while his hands explored her elsewhere. She shuddered when he eventually reached the final destination, and cried out when her time came. When it did, and as he had hoped, Hap found her delicious.

"Oh Hap, this should have happened a long time ago, and you know it, right?"

"Some things are like that, Sunny, but for the record, since the beginning I've tried to remain chaste during the chase."

"And I'm about to chasten you for your resistance to our date with destiny."

"Truth is, since the day we first met I've enjoyed the thrill of every moment's anticipation that one day we'd be locked in body."

"Then let's finish fulfilling those wanton desires."

She rolled Hap onto his back and quickly mounted him before he could offer any protest to her desire for ultimate dominance and supremacy. Immediately finding what she was after, Sunny slowly eased herself into position before her pace quickened as the frenzy took over. Though not without some lower back pain, Hap did his best to further enhance their pairing by fully energizing each of his accompanying upward thrusts to the fullest.

Reaching her second and third zenith before Hap did was something that had never before happened, and Sunny relished the newfound ecstasy. Though fully satisfied in ways she had always hoped for, she didn't want it to end just yet. So, unwilling to disengage from the source of her pleasure, she collapsed on top of him. There she remained until their heart rates returned to normal as their bodies slowly cooled to room temperature.

It was clear Hap was having more than a little difficulty processing what had just happened, and Sunny knew it. She could sense that his passion was ebbing once they were disentangled and she could just stare at him.

"Hap, your pensive look tells me this is the first time you've partaken of the forbidden fruit."

"Am I really that transparent?"

"I've done little else but study you since coming aboard last year and am pretty sure I can read all the telltale signs."

Hap didn't know what he was supposed to feel. He only knew how he felt, and that was something he wasn't proud of. At the very least, it would cast a long shadow on his otherwise unblemished and perfect marriage. After hesitating for a moment before responding, he tried his best at crafting the kind of confession that wouldn't upset her.

"This shouldn't have happened, Sunny, but you and I both know it had to."

"Of course it did, and don't worry – I'm not expecting this to blossom into a future I have no right to and know I never will. Let's just enjoy it for what it is and while it lasts."

"So you wanted to use me but not abuse me?"

"Instead, let's just say I wanted to borrow you, and for one night only."

"Like the fulfillment of a fantasy?"

"There's nothing wrong with fantasies, Hap. In fact, they're fairly normal and necessary for maintaining a healthy sexual appetite. I don't mean to trivialize what just happened, but for me it helps solve my infatuation with you."

Sunny hadn't always been so forward, but the technique had been well honed over a number of years as she evolved into an accomplished aggressor. The conversion began in her teens when, like most teenage girls, she was curious, but not promiscuous. That too would change. Her loss of innocence began in the back seat at a drive-in theatre when a junior in high school. Though she saw very little of it that night, *Doctor Zhivago* was a very long movie that could have provided ample time for a proper introduction to intimacy and extended seduction, but didn't.

Before then she had only ever been to second base and figured that was far enough at her age. Plus, Sunny had an older brother who had warned her repeatedly about what to expect from boys in that situation. He no doubt knew from experience what it was like to be stranded on base. Nevertheless, that night she rounded third on the fly and headed for home plate. To her credit, she hadn't planned to go all the way, but once her hormones took over and came to a full boil, the progression was all but unstoppable. Though she hadn't encouraged him, neither had she offered any resistance to the deflowering. She had, however, spent much time regretting it thereafter. In reflection years later she also wondered what parts of the movie she did remember may have played a role in why she would battle the Russians with such vigor and if her resolve was initially rooted in that backseat experience.

The transition from maidenhood to womanhood was supposed to be exhilarating and memorable, but Sunny's was only painful. For her, it was always about being desired and not just "had" or taken. Despite the setting, it had been an opportunity for something tender and nearly sacred to happen. Instead, her careless boyfriend had rushed it along to a fast conclusion that didn't include her own.

When robbed of something so precious, it should not have been by a clumsy thief in a big hurry, but by a patient and sensitive one…maybe someone like Hap Franklin. Of course, there would have been long-term fallout from that too, but of a far different kind. Sunny was certain that if Hap had been the first, he would have spoiled her for all who might follow.

Despite her youth, after *Doctor Zhivago* Sunny was no longer a neophyte, and it showed. She quickly became familiar with the equipment and would need no guidance to make it come alive in ways that pleased its owners. But it wasn't long until she grew tired of taking care of the needs of her partners. Instead, she began using men only for her own satisfaction.

That had worked out well for her until the night with Hap in Switzerland, which had been different and threatened to change everything she believed about men. She may not have known it at the time, but after Hap crossed the line that night, she would never again find satisfaction in others who tried in vain thereafter.

# BEYOND THE BRINK

I N SPITE OF NEAR EXHAUSTION following the kind of marathon that defined the night spent together in Sunny's room, both were able to complete their intended mission the next day. And unlike the anguish that would forever follow Hap from the night with Sunny, he had no such reflection in the aftermath of killing the Russian. After all, that was business, and business was, well…just business.

There had been a minor casualty from executing their business, and it was all Hap's fault. When skiing down the mountain, he couldn't resist hotdogging a bit in front of Sunny, which was his nature. Attempting a trail beyond his ability and at a faster speed than practical, he tumbled head over heels and broke his nose. Unable to seek professional treatment for fear of being remembered by the first aid personnel if they were ever questioned when the dead body was eventually discovered, he had to make do with Sunny treating him. She made a cold compress by rinsing a spare sock in the snow, and then mopped-up all the blood from his head and jacket so they could return to their rooms without drawing any unwanted attention.

It reminded him of a similar incident from his adolescence, and also one when he was showing off – that time his ice skating ability for a girl with whom he would forever be smitten. How odd that when love first made itself known to Hap as a youngster, he would never quite shake it off. That was long in the past, and by now he should have outgrown it, but he hadn't. Her name was

Louise, and now Dr. Louise Porter, though close friends were given to calling her Weezie.

Curiously, Weezie had done the very same thing as Sunny when Hap had broken his nose that first time in junior high. Taking charge by repeatedly daubing his nose with her knee sock until the bleeding stopped had seemed such a natural response. In life's rearview mirror, Hap now treasured the memory as one of the seminal moments in what eventually would become an even more complicated past with Louise Porter, M.D.

Sunny insisted Hap lie down with his head elevated until the pain ceased. While he dozed, she packed both their suitcases for the planned departure. But before he awoke, and as if to further punctuate what remained of their time together, Sunny climbed aboard and teased him into repeating what they had done so well the night before. Though knowing he shouldn't, Hap obliged her with another performance that even surprised him. After that day, he would not see Sunny Day for another twenty years, and though alone with his guilt, neither would he ever forget what it had been like with her.

Kate was Hap's wife, true love and life partner. She had set his heart afire from the beginning, and continued to do so long after her death. Like most men, there had been times when his allegiance to her had been challenged, but not violated. However, it had never before been tested by someone like Sunny, and that time he failed. Torn between fidelity and passion, Hap had made the wrong choice and was no longer an exemplar of virtue.

Even for a man whose job it was to tell lies for a living, he knew the difference between a little white lie and a bald-faced one. Deceit should have been something he practiced only when demanded by his side work as an undercover operative. At Langley, he had been decorated at the highest levels for his duplicitous tradecraft, including one medal bestowed by the president himself in the Oval Office. But given that the awards were for trickery, lying and killing, it had always seemed odd to Hap that such laudatory ceremonies celebrated something he wouldn't otherwise consider a worthy or customary element of his character. His rationale for taking the life of another was that such a trespass was sanctioned by duty and a sense of justice, but that was becoming increasingly harder to justify.

Maybe he had since grown hardened to the reality of deceit and, over time, had begun to ignore and even accept its implicit dangers. The dalliance with Sunny was the perfect example of such deterioration. That time Hap had crossed the line into a category called sin, and because it was one of those that began with *thou shalt not*, he knew full well it was an especially egregious one. Sins of the flesh had always been and likely always would be the most popular, but that didn't mean they were any less forgivable.

Unlike communion or baptism, penance wasn't one of the sacraments routinely celebrated by most folks. Those who did made only an abbreviated effort and were thereby due a similarly sized small blessing of forgiveness. That reluctance to experience suffering comparable to the sin committed was no doubt why some enterprising Catholic Church leaders began peddling indulgences in the Middle Ages. But atonement wasn't that simple. Beyond paying a token temporal penalty to excuse the sin, it demanded genuine sacrifice by the supplicant. To Hap's credit, he knew the Almighty was nobody's fool and rightfully expected far more from sinners in the way of ongoing penance.

One of these days he would work his way through all ten commandments one at a time, but now wasn't the time. Hap had never lied to Kate and, at the time, prayed he would never have to. Fortunately he hadn't, but ever since had borne the weighty burden of the transgression alone. Hap would forever consider it of such magnitude that he was unable to seek forgiveness by sharing it with God. Plus, in spite of his unwillingness to take it upstairs in prayer, he was sure the Almighty was already aware of the trespass and would patiently be awaiting Hap's plea for a pardon upon arrival.

# FACETS

T HE NEXT FEW DECADES THAT FOLLOWED his encounter with Sunny had been challenging. The Lord made sure Hap's plate was always full by dishing out an overbrimming daily ration of trials and opportunities. Fortunately, Hap had two speeds – fast and faster. Though not always warranted, he had a sense of urgency about every last chore on his daily "to do" list. Balancing work and play involved more apprehension and tension than it should have. True to his Pennsylvania Dutch roots, work always came first. Play was reserved for what little time remained after the hay was in the barn. After all, there was a reason it was called work.

Differentiating the wheat from the chaff had been a struggle in itself. Hap labored tirelessly in pursuit of the momentous instead of stopping long enough to savor the uncomplicated happiness that life afforded every day. Motivated by a touch of the "Savior Complex" probably kept him from becoming a better version of himself. It also provided the ammunition for Hap's odd but routine way of sanctifying his decisions. Misguided priorities usually kept him from confronting what should have been his life's real work, though one day down the road and with the benefit of hindsight he would learn that lesson the hard way.

Hap also liked to win, and win big. Losing was never an option, and giving up in futility was equally anathema. Simply put, he was a gracious winner, but a sore loser. Though the instances in the loss column were rare, when they occurred he always got even. Keeping his nose affixed to the grindstone paid off with a slew of successes, but those accomplishments also tended to validate some of the disagreeable idiosyncrasies that got him to that place. His routines often got in the way and there were casualties along the journey, though probably far fewer if Kate hadn't done her best to keep him within the guardrails of normalcy. This was no secret to most of Hap's old friends, who knew that Kate had single-handedly re-engineered his personality into a more acceptable range of public tolerance.

Another underlying trait was that Hap was always in a hurry. Never forgetting his grandmother's warning that idle hands would assuredly be assigned to the Devil's workshop, he kept busy at all times. More so than most, he knew that theft of time reduced productivity, so it wasn't surprising that his work ethic extended to the way Hap worked best at Sterling Capital Management.

For example, there should have been plenty of space for visitors in Hap's spacious and sumptuous mahogany-paneled office, but he fixed that. Over the years he had amassed a collection of variously sized belting leather briefcases, all of which came in handy to fix the problem. He got into the habit of intentionally stacking the briefcases together with an assortment of client files on the couch and in every chair. With nowhere to sit, this discouraged his colleagues from dropping by and wasting Hap's precious time with mindless idle chatter about sports, the market, or office gossip. Soon everyone got the message that Hap's office was not a comfortable place of refuge. Nor was it ever a place to shoot the bull. Because all visitors had to remain standing, bona fide meetings with Hap were brief and personal ones a rarity. The biggest benefit was that the time wasters kept their distance and eventually stopped coming around altogether. That in itself was a blessing.

From all outward appearances, Hap was generally thought of as an extroverted and gregarious guy, but that was another of his disguises. Actually, unless when playing the big room, he preferred keeping his own company, which was yet another secret he kept from all others. Though most knew that beyond his humor, thrift was the centerpiece of his identity, the few who got to peek behind the curtain found him generous and never stingy when it came to picking up a dinner tab or helping others in need – sometimes in a very big way. Those closest to Hap respected the many unselfish ways he lived his life. No doubt some found him a good example to follow, but perhaps a few others weren't convinced, though probably due to harboring a tinge of jealousy.

Even Hap's full name was more or less a secret, though having nothing to do with maintaining secrecy as a spy. Early in his youth he had largely abandoned his given name – not as a rebuke, but due to its unnecessary complexity. Once a nickname used only at home by his parents, his now commonplace handle of Hap had evolved from the original fully christened one of Benjamin Harrison Franklin. Obvious that he couldn't get through life as Ben Franklin, he had first tried B. Harrison Franklin, but then dropped the B. Because Harrison sounded a bit haughty and had proven to be a real mouthful for his childhood friends, he eventually shortened it altogether to just Hap. It was that final iteration that stuck for life, and only a few of his earliest playmates remembered that it may have been shortened from his nursery name of Happy, which it was. Its brevity suited him and at the same time affirmed his underlying affability. How odd that some parents' choices when naming their offspring were sometimes both prescriptive and predictive, since people often would become what they were named.

Despite his penchant for privacy, some of Hap's other aspects were readily evident to all who took note. No matter how calculating, he probably took too many risks. The financial ones had all paid off big time, whereas the interpersonal ones maybe not so much. Such high stakes gambling may have been rooted in his view that everything in life was a competition and the journey an uphill slog. He enjoyed the allure of taking on risk, and at the very least, embracing such an attitude kept him from seeing his risk-taking as a shortfall instead of a triumph.

Like a poorly cut stone, the brilliance of one facet could be diminished by the flawed opaqueness of another. But in his case, all sides were essential to the whole and worthy of examination to understand the unfinished puzzle otherwise known as Hap Franklin. Unfortunately few beyond Kate, and later Weezie, understood that.

# RIGHTING THE WRONG

H AP HAD RESISTED AUTHORITY FOR A LONG TIME AND couldn't help it. When at odds with laws and regulations, he viewed them as mere guidelines to be obeyed only when they suited him. There were exceptions, like the mandates of his father, whose rule was absolute. Others were the guiding principles he had followed since his time at the University of Virginia, which once was more or less governed by honor and a proper sense of decorum. But like so many things in life that had lost their fascination, propriety and honesty were no longer the revered hallmarks of virtuous behavior he had experienced as a student.

Ignoring the official playbook didn't mean Hap could be compromised. He knew right from wrong, even when it required some of the latter to affirm the former. An example would be the taking of a life to spare another, or in most cases many others. At first it seemed fair enough to justify what he had to do when taking on a CIA side job and was not all that troublesome. After all, he hadn't sought such an unconventional calling. Instead, it had been Bud Smith, together with some help by the then sitting president, who eventually convinced Hap that he was destined for such work. Nevertheless, he couldn't help but view his targets as victims as well, which was why Bud had to keep reminding Hap that they all had it coming to them – if not for the transgression so accused, then for others Langley was unaware of. But after a while the often gruesome side work became a rocky journey of faith. Making that treacherous trek was probably what kept

Hap from becoming unglued, so he suspected God was far from finished with him.

Kate had been gone for nearly a decade, and there was nothing Hap could do to soften the sorrow. There were plenty of substitutes that sustained him along the way, like his children and granddaughter. Eventually there was also Weezie. In their own ways, all of them made the heartache easier to bear, but nothing could fill the void left in his calcified heart after his wife's death. Though that had been the euphemism used publicly when referring to her passing, it hadn't been an ordinary death, but a contract killing. It was all but certain that Kate's murder had been ordered by the Russian president, or Czar, as he was known by all the Western alliance intelligence services.

The burden was an especially heavy one for Hap because he knew the hit on Kate was in retaliation for something he himself had done as an assassin in service to his country. Even in its heavily redacted form, the CIA's file on Kate's death would never see the light of day. That much was understandable and generally the case when proof of culpability involved a head of state. But when the target was a United States citizen killed on American soil, such particulars were reserved for only Langley's seventh floor brass and the commander in chief himself.

Hap had always been a strong believer in fair play, but also subscribed to evening the score through the taking of an eye for an eye taken. Seeking revenge was one thing – emerging successful was quite another, especially when the one he was after was a world leader whose safety was taken very seriously by a virtual army of bodyguards. When it involved his survival, the Czar left nothing to chance. It was common knowledge that when away from his office or residence, he used only his own solid gold port-a-potty when nature beckoned. Before he sat, the seat was scrubbed for any toxins that shouldn't have been there. The notion of taking him down while on the throne was one that Hap found both enticing and entertaining to ponder. Though penetrating the Czar's seemingly impregnable private security detail seemed ludicrous, that hadn't stopped Hap from thinking about it night and day.

No matter how hard he strategized, Hap couldn't devise a scenario that wouldn't involve help from Langley. Officially, he figured securing such assistance wasn't possible, but going it alone as a rogue ex-covert agent would never work. Though having the means, he couldn't replicate the kind of vast network required to execute such a daunting and daring hit. There was only one trustworthy person at the CIA with whom he could even broach the subject, and that was Bud Smith. One of only a few at the agency who had managed to maintain a permanent alias, Hap knew Bud Smith wasn't his real name, but its simplicity seemed to suit him.

Over the years the two had become much more than colleagues. In fact, their relationship was more akin to an abiding friendship. Bud had recruited Hap, functioned as his handler for a time, and eventually rose through the ranks to occupy one of the coveted seventh floor offices. There were now five major directorates at Langley, but only one was charged with the spooky stuff – the Directorate of Operations. As the Deputy Director of Operations, or DDO, Bud was the head of all clandestine and often illegal activity. From the beginning, with Bud as his minder, Hap's success had become near folklore across the spectrum of counterintelligence services. Though he never gloated about it, the notoriety eventually made him harder to manage when in the field.

Like the old days when they both operated in the shadows, Hap would take the plan to Bud in confidence and hope for the best. Such an audacious and certainly off-book operation would have to be sanctioned by the DDO, but might have to be kept secret from any others to provide Bud plenty of cover and, if necessary, impunity if ever discovered. Since there was no reason to delay any longer, Hap set out for Washington. The four-hour jaunt was made easier by taking the Porsche 911 Turbo Cabriolet, which mostly drove itself while permitting Hap time to prepare his case.

The first checkpoint at Langley was unmanned and served only to identify and permit entrance of pre-authorized vehicles equipped with a dashboard-mounted transponder. It was not much different than paying road and bridge tolls on the fly with an EZ-Pass. Fortunately, when Hap had retired the security folks were more lax and somehow had forgotten to confiscate and de-activate his gizmo. The second barrier to entry involved personal inspection and verification of identity. Upon arrival at the gated and armed entrance, he stopped at the station, jumped out and with a genuine smile, extended an outstretched handshake to the familiar guard on duty. Fortunately, it was a man he had known for years and with whom Hap had a good history.

"Hello, Teddy; hope all is well."

"And a hearty homecoming welcome home to you, Mr. Franklin. I don't remember seeing your name on today's guest list, so let me look again."

The approved list, once on a clipboard, had long ago been re-placed by a computer screen, which Hap knew didn't make it any more secure or legitimate than the old method.

"You won't likely find my name on the list, Teddy, as today's visit is an unofficial one with folks on the seventh floor who prob-ably want to keep it off the record. I'm also running a little late and you know how those people hate to be kept waiting."

"Not a problem, Mr. Franklin, go right through and feel free to park in the front row reserved for big shots like them...and you of course."

Only after parking did Hap call the unlisted number every agent knew by heart. As always, it was answered on the first ring.

"Password?"

"Cavalier."

After repeating verbatim a non-sensical sentence spoken by the woman on the other end, she announced that the voice recognition was complete, and asked how she might direct his call.

"Bud Smith, please."

"Right away, Cavalier."

Bud answered himself and with typical abruptness.

"One of these days I'm gonna change the unlisted number needed to reach me so old broken down retirees like you will leave me alone."

"Eventually you'd miss me, Bud, and besides, I'm too old to memorize a new number."

"Yeah, I'd miss you like a fuckin' root canal."

"Well today you're in luck, as I can make that happen right now."

"Whaddaya mean – a root canal or are you just hoping for a visit?"

"I'm outside in the parking lot, but could be in your office within minutes if you give me clearance."

"Christ, how'd you get into the compound to begin with?"

"The guard recognized me and waved me on through; see, it helps to be a popular living legend driving a fancy car."

"Still breaking the rules, huh? Well fine, come on up, I'll have Patti clear you for entry."

"For years now I've been hoping she would do just that."

The protocol for admission had advanced since his last visit. Beyond the usual and mundane credentials like ID and password, the procedure included a full body bionic scan to confirm facial and retinal identity. Since the evolution of biometric data collection, or essentially hacking human beings in all manner of innovative ways, had become standard in the new era of security, Hap supposed there was no reason Langley need to refrain from using it on its own inmates. Though intended to ensure the invulnerability of the top brass, the procedure nevertheless made Hap feel more vulnerable. Once identities were confirmed, even someone like Hap was subjected to a thorough swabbing of his clothing to sniff-out any trace of things that shouldn't be present. Only then was he escorted by a burly armed guard to the hallowed seventh floor where the top dogs ruled.

Bud's longtime assistant, Patti, was clearly overjoyed to see her one-time favorite operative. Excitedly jumping to her feet, she delivered Hap a smooch, but this time on the mouth and not the cheek as had always been her greeting before.

"Oh, Hap, I've missed you and, frankly, so has the Boss, though he might be loath to admit it."

"Yeah, he's never been one for expressing sentiment, but I'm glad to know you're the touchy-feely kind."

"You have no idea, but I so wish you did."

"Sometimes speculation alone can be more enticing than reality."

"Just so you know, I can always make that dream come true."

"Thanks for that confession, Patti; that'll keep me going for a long time to come and warm during cold winter nights after pulling the covers up."

"So, will we be fitting you for a new cape today or does the old one still fit?"

"Truth is, I'd like to keep the old one, but like everything else in my wardrobe, it's gotten tight during the pandemic."

"Maybe I could let it out for you during a personal fitting."

"Why how accommodating you are. I never would have guessed, and just so you know, for an adjustment like that I could be available most anytime."

"See, I've been telling you for years that membership here has its privileges."

"But beyond you, damn few upside benefits."

"By the way, our new cape is the go-to choice of all the best spies; it's essentially the Bugatti of undercover loungewear."

"But I don't wear much under the covers."

As was his custom, Bud had been listening all along until their playful banter had become a bit too serious and he felt it was now time to interrupt. As he had done many times before, Bud punctuated his disapproval with the typical admonishment issued in his customary booming voice.

"Hey, knock it off out there. You two sound like stray dogs in heat. Hap, get your sorry ass in here before I have to turn the fire hose on both of you."

As Hap entered the spacious inner sanctum of the Deputy Director, he saw that little had changed beyond the absence of smoke and acrid scent of stale cigarette butts. The place was a combination of neatly stacked files on the floor and a total disarray of far too much paperwork atop the huge desk and conference table. It was the way Bud had always worked, and given his ascendency to the seventh floor, his preference for clutter and disorganization had seemed to work for him.

While raising his bushy eyebrows, Bud immediately held up his index finger, which meant silence was to be maintained surrounding what he expected would be the real purpose of Hap's visit. Hap instinctively understood the signal, and they continued what amounted to only pleasantries and idle conversation until Bud arose and headed for the door.

"Come take a walk with me, Hap. I need a cigarette and last year this place went smokeless, even here on the seventh floor. The new director is a fuckin' health nut and hasn't figured out that smoking, like playing with guns, is an essential part of our tradecraft here."

"And probably not as dangerous to your health, right?

"I have no clue, but do need my daily overdose of nicotine and caffeine just to focus on what keeps me awake at night."

"And here I thought there was nothing that frightened you."

"Nothing but the specter of your visit today, but we'll get to that soon enough once we're outside."

As they passed through Patti's outer office, she couldn't resist teasing them.

"Oh, out for a little fresh air again so soon, Boss? Why don't you leave Hap here with me? I'll take good care of him until you return."

"That's what I'm afraid of. Plus, this place is probably bugged, and I'd be hard pressed to explain away a video of you two engaged in a little sport-fucking on my couch."

"I've always hoped for a screen test, but at my age wasn't planning to leave the lights on during filming."

As she'd hoped, Patti's comments brought a good laugh from both the spymaster and his one-time master spy. After exiting the building, Hap knew where they were headed. Because some conversations at Langley had to be private, there was ample green space surrounding the building for what in CIA parlance was called a "stroll". Though the participants were identifiable by sight, what was discussed on a stroll was not privy to any stray passersby or electronic eavesdropping.

Given Hap's notoriety, he was recognizable by most of the others who were out for a stroll. Obeying the unofficial protocol, most kept their distance, but a few couldn't resist the urge to acknowledge, wave or greet Hap by name. Perhaps by doing so, some hoped a little of his magic might rub off on them. Though legendary, many of the stories about Hap that still made the rounds here were downright apocryphal, and he knew that.

His experience and reputation alone had given Hap plenty of opportunity for gravitas when commanding some of the operatives that called Langley their second home, but he never chose to embrace it. Rather, when befriending what could sometimes be a disobedient band of ragtag followers, he had typically relied on humor when setting an example. For the most part, such a disarming strategy had worked for him in all walks of life. Plus, he enjoyed sharing parts of the comedic canvas of his own life.

Like he had done when exiting Sterling Capital, Hap had once vowed never to return here. Nevertheless, it felt like a homecoming. Despite what the others may have guessed about his visit, Hap was not here for a reunion, but only to seek Bud's complicity in what Hap was planning for the Czar. When far from the others, they finally sat on a limestone bench next to an upright ashtray expressly installed to accommodate Bud's habit.

"So tell me, Hap, how is it on the other side of retirement?"

"To tell the truth, there are days when I wish I'd never left the circus."

"I'm praying this isn't one of those days, because I have a sneaking suspicion about what you came here to discuss, and it isn't my health. So before you start, the answer is *no*."

"You're not *that* clairvoyant, Bud."

"Oh I think so, and especially this time, which, by the way, isn't the time to be going after the Czar."

"Well, when *is* the right time?"

"Not *any* time under my watch."

"Bud, I really think it's possible to take him out."

"Oh just great, because so far, nobody else does."

"I've got a plan, but I'll need your help."

"Jesus, Joseph and Mary, Hap – just leave it alone. I can't and won't be the scapegoat if this little caper of yours goes sideways. I'm almost ready to turn in my paperwork to retire, and getting caught up in something like this could get me discharged without benefits."

"Or get you a medal in a very private ceremony at the White House. Look, Bud, the new guy on Pennsylvania Avenue understands the Czar and gets it. He'd be thrilled if the bastard gets what's coming to him instead of only slapped with an unending stream of unenforceable tariffs and sanctions."

"Not in this case. I've done the dance with POTUS before, and unlike the last one, our new commander in chief plays by the rules. Believe me, he won't want to know anything about this in order to disavow any involvement by Team USA."

"I suppose he's busy worrying about the other lunatic in North Korea or how we get out from under China's vise-like grip on our economy."

"All that and a lot more, but let's face it, China already owns our ass."

"Bud, you gotta believe this delicate equilibrium we have with the Russkies and Chinese is simply not sustainable."

"I share your paranoia, which may be overblown. Then again, it's not like either side signed a prenup governing future behavior."

"But we gotta start somewhere, and damn soon, so just hear me out before you throw me out."

Hap unveiled the granular details of his plan while Bud listened without interrupting and as was typical, with his eyes closed and head bowed. Well aware it was the only way Bud could concentrate, Hap left nothing out, hoping the allure of a good operation would prove irresistible. When finished, Hap knew the silence that followed was a clear sign that Bud was intrigued by the proposed caper. Finally, Bud raised his head and spoke.

"First, the sublimity alone of your plan is attractive for all the right reasons."

"And also reasonable in its simplicity."

"Look Hap, as with other ideas you've conjured up in the past, I like it, but that doesn't mean I'm willing to buy it."

"I'll take that as a good start, but not yet a yes."

"I probably shouldn't tell you, but we've been planning for something like this for years and even have an operational code name for it – *Bad Bear Down*."

"That's hardly a surprise, as I suspect since first taking your mother's milk you've spent most waking moments conspiring about all kinds of things."

"Well, the red tape to get this done was a bigger surprise to us than we thought, so my written analysis will have to be carefully nuanced. Beyond POTUS's eyes, the circle involves the State Department, Pentagon, and probably a nebby Congressional oversight committee."

"And do you have them all singing from the same hymnbook yet?"

"For obvious security reasons, they can't be read in just yet; for now it's been limited to oblique conversations with the president. Problem is, like any beleaguered first-termer hoping for a second, he's got enough on his plate without inviting more pushback from the leftover party members of his predecessor."

"Luckily for you, this one's capable of keeping his mouth shut."

"Though a bureaucrat for sure, like most before him, I think the president fancies himself a wannabe spy, and believe me, Hap, they all do once they're in the Oval. Anyway, at least this one sees all the others in uniform as support for what Langley does best, so I think we can count on special treatment while granted the odd and unusual favors from the military."

"It's always easier for us when the others play nice and understand who's behind the wheel."

"That hasn't always been the case. You have no idea what I have to deal with. Most of the aging upper echelon at the Pentagon think we should nuke North Korea back to the stone age and let whatever's left all alone to create a new civilization. Of course, these decrepit war hawks consider what Johnson did by pulling the plug in Vietnam to have been a mistake too."

"I suppose it's tough being an old soldier with nobody to fight. All of those generals are veterans of lost wars and are itching to win one before they're forced to mothball their uniforms."

"I don't have to remind you that the military doesn't have much love for us. If we were to bring down a tyrant like the Czar and communism along with him, they'd be more than jealous. And believe me, it wouldn't be long until they try to get even in some roundabout way."

"We can't worry about that now, Bud. Infighting within the beltway will always be a constant. Let's just get it done."

"There's one thing that could be a big problem if I bring you in on this."

"A problem for you or me?"

"Both of us, Hap. Getting you into the country is easy, but you'd be under the direction of our station chief in Moscow."

"That's understood, so what's your hesitancy?"

"Obviously you don't know, but the new station chief is Sunny Day."

"Oh. Really?

"Yes, really."

"Well, I can work under her."

"That's what I'm afraid of, Hap."

"C'mon, we put that to bed a long time ago."

"And because of that you two might get sloppy, take your eyes off the ball, and put it to bed again."

"Good grief, Bud, I'm getting more of that than I can handle from the good Dr. Porter, and why on earth would I ever put that relationship in jeopardy?"

"I'm more worried about Sunny than you."

"How so?"

"Look, she's as good an agent as I've ever had in the field, and you should know because you trained her. But there are two things you may not know – she's still single and as ravishing as you remember her."

"So?"

"There may be a big reason she's single. According to our shrinks, that's because she's never quite gotten over you."

"That's *her* problem."

"No, it's mine, but it'll be yours if I greenlight this."

"When might that be?"

"Give me a few days to think it through and I'll be back in touch."

Hap presumed that most western intelligence services had formed similar contingency plans for the Czar as well, but few had the balls to advance them. More so than in other countries, in America such an action would be under examination and scrutiny by all sides of the political spectrum. Further goading the DDO wasn't going to be helpful, and Hap would have to stand down until a decision was forthcoming. Hesitation in the face of adversity wasn't something Hap was very good at keeping under control. He was equally unprepared for handling the other temptation.

# MISSTEPS APLENTY

H AP HAD ENOUGH ON HIS PLATE without the added burden of anguishing over sins of the past, especially the one involving Sunny Day. He knew it didn't have to happen the way it did, but it had. Life was designed by God to include failure, and Hap assumed that his long-ago romp with Sunny was one of those occasions. After years of regret, he hoped he had put it out of his mind forever, but that wasn't the way sin worked. Instead, it gnawed away at the soul like a persistent, invasive rodent looking for a permanent home. He was all but certain he had successfully put that memory aside and locked up the accompanying remorse for good. But sin was very serious business, and now that Bud had resurrected the indiscretion, Hap was afraid he would be saddled with renewed psychological fallout from yet one more of his missteps.

Only he, the CIA, and the Lord knew that some of his transgressions had been more than missteps. Despite his abiding reverence for life, Hap had made exceptions while in harness to his second master – the worldly one charged with keeping America safe from what could go bump in the night. Though he was not always the one who pulled the triggers, Hap had taken life from more targets than he wanted to remember. The big problem for him now was learning to forget them and forgive himself.

When confronting everything else that had given him pause before, he would apply the same remedy – navigate through the darkness and stare it down. Despite such conviction, he knew this time may demand more than his usual brand of self-medication and convalescence under his own care. Since life was universally considered a God-given gift, extinguishing it was supposed to be a decision reserved only for the Almighty. Violating that assuredly made him a first-rate sinner. On the bright side, it was a good thing Hap wasn't Catholic, as any priest would have fallen asleep in the confessional if forced to hear the litany of all his sins.

The long-running saga of Hap and Louise Porter, also fondly known as Weezie by those closest to her and further shortened to the single-syllabled "Weeze" by Hap, had only reached midstream. Rooted in adolescence, their mutual attraction had blossomed into a passion neither of them could have anticipated. When fate had thrown them together while planning a high school reunion, they were both vulnerable, and that's how it all began. Though once separated by time and space, following that reunion they became strangers no more.

With Hap grieving the loss of his wife, Kate, at the same time Weezie was trying to escape from an ill-fated third marriage to a powerful Russian oligarch. Hap's role in making that separation happen had taken a few years, but was ultimately successful. Ridding themselves of the oligarch known as Dmitri Cherkov was a long story in itself and of the kind found only in the very best of books. The short version was that once the Russkie was brought down and out of the picture, though not assuredly eliminated, Louise was ready and anxious to move along with Hap. So far it had been an exceptional relationship, as each completed and enabled the other. One impediment stood in her way; Weezie could tell that Hap still carried a torch for Kate. Even more dangerous was that he was consumed by avenging her murder.

Hap wasn't the kind of man who could leave things unsettled, especially something like the hit on his wife ordered by the Kremlin. His escalation of hatred for the Russian president had long passed the point where Hap could control it, and he craved a rightful retribution. He also knew that any chance of self-transcendence would be as the result of his own direct involvement in what had to be a grisly and punishing death of the Czar. One by one Hap had destroyed all the other participants involved in the plot to kill Kate, leaving the most challenging target for last.

Much of the happiness Hap had enjoyed since Kate's murder was attributable to his reconnection with Weezie, especially after so many decades of being all but strangers. She was an enchantment like no other that he had awakened from. Once reunited, and against insurmountable odds, their love had flourished. In itself an exciting epic, the story of Hap and Louise was a complex one in constant search of a happy ending. It was also the kind of story that only Hap could tell, and perhaps one day he would. Beyond chronicling their transformative relationship, maybe he would try his hand at fashioning it into a novel once life slowed down and he finally had time to do what he had always wanted. It might become his magnum opus, but for now he was all but consumed by demons over Kate's killing. Plus, because writing was a lonely and solitary activity where the work was done in private, Hap wasn't sure he wanted to go underground for such an extended stay. To really thrive, he had always needed an audience, but for several years now, it had been Weezie alone as his sole muse in a front row seat.

Though both were now convinced they were destined to be together since the seventh grade, the practicality of making their union a legally-binding one for all time was problematic. The celebrated career of Dr. Louise Porter, M.D. was approaching, but hadn't yet reached its potential, so it wouldn't make sense for Weezie to leave Johns Hopkins just yet. Also, apart from being a world renowned behavioral psychologist nearing the peak of her game, Weezie's real tie to Baltimore was that both of her daughters had settled there, and she relished the luxury of remaining very involved in their lives.

Pragmatic to the core, Hap was equally reluctant to abandon the familiar, comfortable, and special place the privileged

Pittsburgh enclave known as Fox Chapel was for him. They had managed to skirt the issue far longer than they should have, but that was the way they were put together. It was not an uncommon predicament, and as with many other couples on the fence, may have driven them closer together. Besides, their routine of seeing each other two weekends a month was likely more satisfying than if they had to put up with one another full-time under one roof.

For Weezie, Hap's luster had always been sparkling and bright, if not alluring. Though some of his facets were tarnished and opaque, they couldn't diminish his overall vitality for life or her lifelong attraction. Despite a mutual fascination that began in junior high school, somehow they had never hooked up over the intervening years, notwithstanding occasional opportunities to do so. When they finally had, it was satisfying in ways neither could have imagined.

Sure, he was flawed, though not in ways she couldn't repair. She dealt with defective personalities every day and saw each one as a personal challenge. With lots of clinical experience now under her belt and proven remedies in her tool kit, she was eager to begin that work by releasing and illuminating Hap's inner uncut brilliance. Weezie knew he would be resistant to change, but not if she were patient with her patient and doled out a quid pro quo of affection as compensation.

# UNNECESSARY BURDENS

T HE FEDERAL GOVERNMENT WAS SLOWLY MAKING THE turn from sloth and greed to productivity and parity that benefitted the entire nation. Once genuine patriots took the places of the sycophants appointed by the prior administration, meaningful forward progress was already apparent, at least to all who could see it without political blinders.

Internally, America was most weary of two things – the pandemic and politics. The pandemic was manageable and had, for the most part, passed, but the political shenanigans would not. One side embraced the standard-issue authoritarian playbook used by all despots – consolidate and control power by preying upon the weakest and dumbest, ignoring the needy, and disenfranchising the rights of any dissenting voters. Once the stage was set for unyielding polarization among the disparate factions, it was easy to divide and conquer the electorate by pitting the most energized against their fellow countrymen. Though hardly a new paradigm, it still worked, even in what the world would have expected to be the most enduring model of democracy.

In a last ditch effort to seize ultimate power, America's last president went so far as to single out and enlist his followers to commit anarchy against their own flag. Though unremarkable in every way and rarely doing anything unless there was something in it for him financially or politically, he was a master at mobilizing a mob. Even after their failed attempt at insurrection and years after he left office, his rabid supporters continued to denounce the election results that toppled their party's messianic leader, confirming their well-deserved further descent into asininity. Their ongoing collective assaults on democracy were flagrant, destructive and contagious, but not crippling. The rest of the world watched and worried, wondering how so many could have been duped by such a big lie.

Nevertheless, and though his influence was waning, the former president remained a potent internal threat to the country. As odious as his behavior was, it proved tedious and expensive to convict him of the many high crimes he had committed both in and out of office. After being turned away by the voters, he couldn't resist stoking the fires of insurgency by spewing ongoing falsehoods. Deceit, fraud and fabrication, especially when coupled with his unbridled arrogance, had previously been something only possible by foreign dictators and witnessed from afar. Now that it had arrived on the shores of America the Beautiful, maybe the real foe all along was the enemy within. Hopefully, there would be a vigorous pushback by the majority to resist despotism and restore the will of the people.

Externally, Uncle Sam was in double jeopardy. Of its two primary adversaries capable of destroying democracy, it was the Russians who were more apt to commit blatant aggression. The Czar's unprovoked utter destruction of Ukraine was the most recent testament, but not his primary target. He was hell-bent on ruining America and all it stood for as fast as possible, whereas the enlightened Chinese had a long-term plan that was far better.

Economically, the United States was already held hostage as the leading captive consumer of China's prodigious output of goods and services. While patiently stealing its technology, buying its real estate, and acquiring much of the world's natural resources, The People's Republic nurtured it's desired prey along a path guaranteeing that America would continue nursing from China's bosom forever. Ideological differences aside, what all the Communists really coveted was America's relative prosperity.

But unlike Russia, it was the farsighted Chinese who understood that coercive economic tactics trumped outright warfare.

They were also a patient people, and accustomed to having time on their side. As the oldest civilization that could boast of a written history, the Chinese already had withstood more than three thousand years of warfare. With such unmatched history and experience behind them, they could afford to sit back and await the failure of democracy so that their ultimate dominion of the world could occur without needless bloodshed.

For Hap, there were increasingly more things that were scary, but his own survival wasn't necessarily one of them. Foreign economic domination might be manageable under the right conditions, so at this point, he was focused more on outcomes that would be far worse, like the possible doomsday scenarios facing his children and their progeny.

Nuclear disarmament had been nothing but an agenda item for all the worldwide summits held since the obliteration of Hiroshima and Nagasaki. Instead, for an entire generation, the major global powers poured far too much of their GNP into developing even more powerful weapons capable of world-wide annihilation. These efforts were both overt and covert. In America, the mere existence of the most sophisticated weaponry was revealed only to the president and a handful of politicians. Had those vast resources pissed away on warfare been committed instead to eradicating poverty, slowing global warming, and curing cancer, Hap's children might not be suffering from such fears. Nor was he himself immune from the same anxieties, so more frequently than ever before, Hap awoke in a cold sweat, which added credence to the nightmares.

Having reached life's twilight period, Hap was less concerned about how those uncertainties would play out during his own remaining time than he was about how he could confront and manage the despair of his children. It was a tall order, and one for which he had no easy recipe. There were no right answers to annihilationism. One thing was certain – he would willingly sacrifice everything to ease the burden of their apprehensions. Returning to the CIA and taking one last life didn't seem overly troublesome, as he could grapple with the sin later. If it worked, but he didn't make it back, taking the bear down would be worthy of his sacrifice.

So far, immortality was something only Jesus had been able to pull off, and Hap had now reached the age when he hoped he might also be along for the ride. He was not alone in pondering such a thought. In fact, no doubt every soul on earth had fantasized about eternal life at some point. At this stage his peers were fixated on simply extending life instead of embracing it for what it was and taking steps to improve it in preparation for whatever came next. Hap was committed to doing more of that during what time remained, but only after his business with the Czar was finished.

# BELOVED OFFSPRING

TOGETHER, KATE AND HAP had done a good job raising their two children. To be sure, each brought a different dimension to parenting, but somehow it had all worked out well. For things practical or financial, they sought Hap's advice. If it were a pressing, time-sensitive problem, they knew they could always rely on his ability to think the issue through quickly, proffer his guidance, and get them out of any jam in a hurry.

For longer heart-to-heart talks, they instinctively went to their mother. Kate was territorial about her role, never betrayed confidences, and was better than Hap could have been in such circumstances. Though he was a bit jealous of that special connection all children seemed to have with their mothers, he was satisfied with his own separate job as the provider and occasionally the fixer. Curiously, the rapport was not unlike the relationships he and his siblings had experienced with their own parents, which in a way confirmed the old adage about the "sins of the father visited on the children."

Kate was stoic, whip smart, and headstrong…but so was Hap, and as might be expected, the friction between them was dangerously close to ignition. Fortunately, their sparring never became more than just that. For Hap, it had never gone beyond good-natured jousting. Of course, it was now too late to apologize if it had. Nevertheless, if he had it to do over, Hap would have let her win more of the battles no matter how hard the capitulation might test his nature.

By the time of Kate's death, both of the kids had already gone their separate ways and were successful beyond even Hap's lofty expectations. But without Kate as a magnet, now there was at best only half as much reason for them to return home. He had never quite gotten over the necessity of kids having to abandon the nest and replace the nuclear family with an extended one. A hopeless sentimentalist at heart, Hap spent far too much time dwelling on the past, which was no doubt bothersome to those like his children who had more of a future ahead of them.

As their visits grew less frequent, there were times Hap felt like no more than an onlooker from afar. He had never before been an outsider or bystander, but always at the center of the action, so it was a hard transition. There had been occasions when both children found him meddlesome, and at times even quarrelsome. The last thing he wanted to be was an intrusive annoyance in their already complicated lives. After Kate's passing he'd gotten better at being less of a nuisance, or maybe they were more forgiving when he couldn't.

Hap had spent his life trying to make their lives easier, only to finally discover that wasn't what they wanted from him. Though too late to turn back those pages, he hoped there was enough time left on the clock to start afresh. Kate had forewarned him that such a time would come and the regret might be unendurable. He had largely ignored her overtures and was now paying the piper.

Then again, because Hap tended to live in the shadow of every mistake he'd ever made, there was a slight chance he was overthinking it, and this was all imaginary. Nevertheless, and to be safe, he made a solemn self-pledge to repair any worrisome elements of his relationships with the children. And as with any of his other objectives, it would be fostered by inclination achieved through fierce determination. That was the way he did things, and Hap was very set in his ways.

Already aware from Bud that his son, Christian, had made a preliminary inquiry to the CIA about joining the dark side, Hap was fairly sure he could put a stop to that, but then what? Hap couldn't protect his son forever, but only offer his counsel. At a fairly young age, Christian had already made his mark in life with much fanfare, and now longed for something more exciting, but absent the notoriety. For Hap, it was too close to history repeating itself, and sadly, he knew how the story ended.

Though it might be a little touch and go for a while, Hap hoped Christian would come to his senses and choose what mattered most. It was too late for Hap, who had made the same dumb move at about the same age. Regrets? He had more than a few and hadn't yet cleared all the remaining hurdles to get life right before the curtain fell. But if Bud let Hap back into the game long enough to finish the story, he might have a chance to do so.

Daughter Lindsay might prove to be the most difficult to help, at least in the short run. Even as a youngster, she would maneuver through the minutiae of life and was comfortable swimming against its deeper currents. It had not taken her forty years in the wilderness to figure things out. Lindsay had always railed against racism, poverty, and injustice. Now, as an adult, it was evident she was struggling with the futility of planning and executing a life in an uncertain world of even far greater threats posed by novel diseases, climate change, violent crime and possible nuclear annihilation.

Atrocities akin to the Holocaust were being committed around the globe, and due to verifiable reporting in real time, live news of such things instantly reached anyone who cared to know. Absent much filtering by the media, it was difficult to shield those who were the least bit curious about such horrific events, and Lindsay was always among them. Hap feared she was turning fatalistic, and while unable to eliminate the sources of her existential angst, figured it was his job to restore her optimism, bolster her hope and nurture her faith.

Now with her own child to worry about and tend to, Lindsay already had her hands full solving the personal crises du jour. To

Hap, it seemed so unfair that she couldn't enjoy life the way he had in an era of fewer complications. Reflecting those of her generation, she viewed the world as hopelessly chaotic. It was almost as if she were compelled to ponder horrors like the apocalyptic aftermath from the planet's unleashing its full fury for being poisoned by humankind. Sure, there were clear warnings, like prolonged drought, arid landscapes, horrific forest fires, barren farmland, an exponential increase of tornados, and the gradual disappearance of the polar ice caps. It was also no secret that the retaliation by Mother Nature would only strengthen with ongoing pollution and rape of the earth. Too often Lindsay viewed her own personal challenges as insignificant in comparison, and Hap feared the burden for her might become too great.

Too bad it wasn't so for the feckless members of Congress. With so much of their campaign war chests underwritten by energy companies, hastening proven decarbonization efforts wasn't something they dared tackle in earnest. They were betting that neither Lake Meade nor Lake Powell would dry up before the next election cycle, but if so, the thirsty states that shared the Colorado River basin could duke it out by themselves. Perhaps their expectation was that God would buckle under pressure and intervene by granting the western states one last gratuitous reprieve of sorts.

In collaboration with Mother Nature, God's heaven-sent message might come as a harsh warning in the form of torrential rain, unprecedented snow storms, relentless flooding and needless loss of life. But sadly, once the reservoirs were restored to normal levels, the threat would disappear and the country's leadership could focus on something less important. As before the calamity, while paying lip service to improving the path to sustainability of the earth, blanketing the country with solar panels and wind turbines wasn't a solution anyone at Capitol Hill was willing to espouse.

Despite railing at such legislative lethargy, Lindsay never lost her humor. Curiously, that was also how she had become a near icon in the advertising world. Hap attributed her meteoric rise to instinctively knowing not only what was funny, but clever at the same time. Now the creative director for one of the top firms, she encouraged and nurtured its legions of teams around the world, but also made the final decisions as to what was sufficiently imaginative and amusing before launching full-blown multi-million dollar media campaigns. Lindsay had created new branding and reinvigorated old brands with aplomb. Knowing how to motivate skeptical consumers into running right out to buy a given client's products was far beyond guesswork. Though it required lots of prior research, she also had an innate knack of immediately knowing what would resonate with buyers.

The birth of Hap's granddaughter had neither slowed his daughter's pace nor diminished her wit. Unfortunately, he knew the threats that kept Lindsay awake at night were not solvable overnight, or even in her lifetime. Quelling anxieties about uncertainties wasn't as easy as proving the boogey man wasn't real. He wished he could share with her some of the details of his clandestine efforts to fashion a better world on behalf of the country and humanity, but that could not happen, at least not now.

But what he could never reveal was that his side work for the CIA had been responsible for her mother's death, as such a confession would be devastating to both his son and daughter. Because of Hap's past and possible future involvement in bringing down the Russian Bear, he was more worried about their personal safety. He knew from first-hand experience that the worst of enemies always came after the ones you loved. And if so, it would all be his doing...and ultimately his undoing as well. Though worried his plea may fall on deaf ears, Hap's daily petition was to reach a longstanding covenant with God that if his loved ones were kept safe, he would make any bargain...or sacrifice.

# THE GAUNTLET

I T WAS WEEZIE WHO INVITED HAP to join her for an early midweek dinner. The timing would permit both of them to return home at a decent hour, even if the dinner ended with a romp for dessert. In past years when they wanted to hook up it had been pent-up desire that drove such a rendezvous. When those desperate times came and their busy schedules permitted, they would meet halfway between Baltimore and Pittsburgh, often at an eighteenth-century limestone inn. Because she had long considered it their own special place, that's where she suggested they meet.

The two-hour drive gave her plenty of time to plan how she might push Hap for answers to questions he might not be expecting her to ask. The solitude alone was a rarity and welcome relief from the stress of her daily routine. Immersed in uninterrupted thought also brought back a flood of memories which made the time pass quickly. Hap had long been a contradiction, but an intriguing one she could deal with. Since the seventh grade she had enjoyed all sides of him and was still unable to decide which one she preferred. Despite his disparate factions, somehow Hap was able to merge them into a single complementary dimension that seemed to work for him. However, his obsession with righting all wrongs, especially the one involving avenging Kate's murder, had become more than a major distraction from their relationship.

Mindful of her professional calling as a psychologist, at first Weezie had remained only keenly observant, but relatively silent about his complex persona until she thought she had him figured out. Nevertheless, she always felt at a serious disadvantage, as there remained key pieces of his life that were still unknown to her. Like all her patients, Hap's afflictions were mostly self-inflicted and not necessarily benign. Over the last few years she had tried peddling herself as a panacea for all that troubled him, but apparently to no avail. Untroubled by conflict, Hap actually thrived on it. She knew that, but perhaps had underestimated his zeal for adversity of all kinds, including when being threatened by a loved one presumably closest to him. Only occasionally had she ever been flummoxed by her patients' maladies, but Hap's presented a real challenge. Though probably a dangerous move on Weezie's part, maybe it was time she threw down the gauntlet.

It had been some time since they had last seen each other, and it showed. Instead of the usual undercurrent of erotic excitement, an undertow of tension was palpable from the start. In spite of the warm smile, long embrace and furious kiss, Hap suspected there was another reason Weezie wanted to meet. He also dreaded what that something else might be. Somehow he guessed that this conclave would be far different from their typical trysts and not culminate in what had always been the many pleasures of passion. Nevertheless, and to be on the safe side, he had booked a room upstairs just in case. For additional privacy, he reserved and pre-paid for all five of the guest rooms.

Their joint fascination with old, quaint, and small boutique hotels was no doubt rooted in the Cross Keys Inn of their youth. A one-time stage coach stop in Fox Chapel, the long abandoned and ramshackle inn was where their crowd hid out and often played spin the bottle as kids. Star-crossed as they may have been at that age, no matter how hard he tried, whenever it was Hap's turn, the bottle never ended up pointing at Weezie. It was also why Hap had placed the two matching room keys in the middle of their table before Weezie arrived. Once seated, the skeleton keys were impossible to miss, and Weezie's first words were not what Hap expected.

"That's fairly presumptuous – even for you, Hap."

"Nothing like ginning-up a little spontaneous drama to add some zest to dinner."

"It's not fair, and you know it. You can't just bait me with such a tempting lure all the way through dinner."

"First, I don't think anything's unfair or illegal, especially at our ages. I mean – really Weeze, aren't we way past playing hard-to-get? Plus, there are two keys, which means we both get to make the decision."

"And I see they're intentionally crossed…maybe for added significance?"

"Yes, that was deliberate."

"Oh Hap, though it's been decades since we almost kissed at the Cross Keys, I'll admit I wish we had. Maybe the story of our lives would have had a different outcome."

"But maybe not, so I'll take what we have and not wish for the alternative ending. But let's dial it back a bit and start over with my offering you some wine."

"Only if it's my favorite, and you know the buttery Chardonnay I mean."

"Ha! Knowing they wouldn't stock it, I brought a bottle."

"Hap, you never disappoint. I figured you'd bring your A-game tonight."

"For you I always step up my game, but just wait, there's another surprise. I also convinced the owner to close the restaurant to any other diners or overnight guests."

"But why?"

"So we'd be all alone. There's no reason to share a romantic evening with total strangers. Really, Weeze, you should know by now that the element of surprise is baked into everything I do."

"It must be nice to be able to afford whatever you want in life. Such prodigality doesn't come naturally, though, does it?"

"No, lavish extravagance is somewhat of an acquired aspect that I've had to work hard on to fully embrace. It's in the same boat with self-censorship."

"You'll never get a passing grade for that. For a spy, you really do put it all out there for everyone to see, and often for the shock value alone. As your unofficial shrink, I think you do that only because you like to sit back and enjoy the reaction."

"Look, Dr. Porter, I make no apologies for who or what I am, but must admit that you're really pretty good at uncovering this stuff."

"I guess figuring you out is my true calling in life."

"I don't recall calling you, but just so you know, because of my service to the country, I've learned to be content with anonymity."

"I bet it was a hard lesson for you, Hap."

"Maybe, but I do my best to make the necessary distinction between my two lives and the different roles I must play."

"But can you separate and keep them apart in your mind?"

"Only on good days. But sometimes it gets confusing."

"Tell the truth – besides me, are there *really* other people out there who let you get away with being you?"

"Most of them let me get away with most anything. The others…well, they just ignore me."

"Honestly, is there nothing left in life you haven't yet done or can't pretend to do?"

"Truth is, that bucket list is fairly long, but I hope to finish it before the bell tolls."

"For whom? You?"

"Of course, and I'll be listening for it. But back to lists – getting through life one day at a time may be possible for some, but can't be very fulfilling. You need a long-term game plan, and much like a diet, you gotta stick with it."

"Well, Hap, if all those things are so important, I hope you do…even if for your sake alone."

"Let's just order before this conversation takes a bad turn to somewhere we don't want to end up."

"Fine, but don't get cranky with me; you know how I hate a nasty squabble, and you have a built-in penchant for confrontation."

"Really? And here I'd always thought the attraction was limited to my unrestrained bouts of mirth."

"You do have an acerbic wit and infectious laugh, but snickering and giggling through dinner isn't gonna be enough for tonight."

"So I see; then we'd better move along by your deciding what you're having before the waiter's shift is over."

"Okay, since they don't have soft-shell crabs, unless you've had them flown in by drone, I'll have the Coquilles St Jacques with the beet and goat cheese salad."

"How predictable, but I suppose so is my choice of a grilled ribeye with a side of lobster mac and cheese."

"You really should try something more heart healthy, like chicken or fish."

"Gee whiz, Doc, how did I ever manage to reach an age when everything I like isn't good for me?"

"You should be happy you've lived long enough to get diabetes and heart disease."

"Aren't there pills for that now?"

"None that are preventative. Plus, when the dementia sets in, you'll likely forget to take the meds anyway."

"Well then, when the time comes you can get me a pillbox for Christmas. And soon after that it won't be long till you'll have to wipe the dribble from my chin as well."

"Can't say I'd welcome mopping up your drool, Hap. What a scary harbinger of things to come, especially when one of them may require Viagra."

"You know, you shrinks really oughta spend more time researching cures for the body and not the noggin."

"But the brain controls everything else, so the "psycho stuff" as you call it is what prompts folks like you to choose the wrong paths, and like tonight, make bad decisions about what to eat."

"What if it makes me happy?"

"That only works for a while, and you know it."

"Maybe so, but tonight I'm pushing the pleasure button for a short-term fix and pairing my well-marbled ribeye with a bold Cabernet."

"Do you ever listen to *anyone*?"

"Not so much anymore. I've become rather accustomed to self-treatment. Plus, I've gotten along just fine over the years by heeding only my own advice."

"How well I know, but one day you'll run out of self-administered palliative measures that only relieve the symptoms."

"Yeah, but you forget there's no co-pay for self-diagnosis and treatment, which appeals to the all-important element of thrift in my inescapable Pennsylvania Dutch genome."

"Don't you mean frugality? And with equal parts of Scottish and German heritage, that's one hell of a potpourri of DNA strands you've got coursing through those veins."

"It's imbedded in the marrow too, which no doubt accounts for the virtual mélange of warring factions going on inside me. Weeze, you know I generally dislike generalities, but what a relief to know that I can blame *everything* on heredity. So case finally closed, huh?"

"Oh Hap, there's that and so much more in you that could be fixed, but only after several years of therapy. You're close to needing an intervention."

"If it were on Jung's or Freud's couch, I might be hesitant, but I'd be pleased to lie on yours for a couple rounds."

"You'd probably lie there too, at least to yourself."

"Then we could try some form of laying instead."

"One thing's for certain – you're never short on words, especially those of persuasion."

"This time I really had high hopes of talking you into something."

"Oh *that* – the thing we do so well?"

"Yeah, that and maybe something else."

"Oh *really*?"

"I was hoping for more of an emphatic *yes* from you instead."

"You've become too accustomed to getting what you want and when you want it, Hap, so this is what let's call denial therapy."

"So long as its short-lived. You gotta know by now that abstinence only sharpens the appetite. And remember, as Samuel Johnson observed, 'marriage has many pains, but celibacy has no pleasures'."

"Why Benjamin Harrison Franklin, if you keep it up much longer I'll have to put you in time out."

"So you don't want me to keep it up as long as I can?"

"You've never failed me there."

"That's because nobody moves the needle like you."

"Why thank you, Hap – it's nice to hear you say so out loud."

"But don't you want to find out if I've lost some of my mojo and spontaneity?"

"You've never been a slacker in any area, but you *are* incorrigible."

"And just the way you like me. In fact, some say it's a big part of my charm and may be my most endearing quality."

"Really? And you think I'm not on to your schtick after all these years?"

"That's only when posing as a conniving schemer to get what I want and when I want it."

"Seems that's a full-time job for you, Hap, but to be honest, I don't mind pandering to your desires."

"*Now* you tell me!"

"I gotta say you've only come up short with me when it comes to temperance in the bedroom."

"Can't say I'm familiar with that word."

"Which one? Temperance?"

"Yeah, I thought it had something to do with restrictive behavior, like my self-imposed daily limitation of two martinis."

"No doubt. By the way, has anyone else ever told you how good you are at being bad?"

"All the time, and thank you for noticing, as I've been awaiting such approbation for a long time."

"You're welcome."

"Welcome to what? Are we on the same page here?"

"And what page would that be, Hap?"

"Oh, I think you know what's coming next as you're quite the savant in these matters."

"Not today, Romeo, though I'm certain we both could use a little nooky."

"In a perfect world that too would be on my daily diet. Honestly, though, that's okay because I don't know how much more bliss I could endure in one night. Plus, trying to keep up with you in bed at my age is a lot like golf."

"Golf! I thought you didn't play much anymore."

"I don't, and as Lee Trevino said, that's because 'the older I get, the better I used to be.'"

"I'm sure you're still on top of your game, Hap, and at least making whoopee isn't full of cholesterol like that ribeye. But seriously, you do know that one of these days you're gonna run out of chutzpa and stamina, right?"

"I suppose, but in my mind I'll always be able to turn the clock back to a time before the bravado atrophied."

"If that's to a better place and time, I hope it includes me, but for now, I think putting some distance between us is the healthier option."

The silence that ensued seemed longer than it actually was, but lasted long enough for Hap to grasp what he'd miss most about any curtailment of their relationship. Over the years since Kate died, he had depended on Weezie's accessibility for many things. Beyond companionship, friendship, and intimacy, she had resurrected his vulnerability, which would be essential for whatever partnership might be in their future. With her, there was never the underlying apprehension that he felt when engaging with others, who he kept at a distance without their knowing it. She had been his lifeboat, and Hap knew he should have thanked her, but didn't.

"Are you letting me down easy, Weezie?"

"Only until you get past your quest for vengeance against you know who; then we'll see what's left for us."

"And you don't like what we have now?"

"Of course. All I want is to give us a chance at something more."

Hap knew better than to cue-up yet another flippant response, and instead kept his mouth shut for a change. He also expected his silence would bring her around as it always had. When it didn't, he finally answered, but again with another question.

"And what would that be?"

"I need some clarity about us, like what's the sequel beyond getting into my pants."

"How about I tell you when the time comes?"

"You're being evasive again, Mr. Franklin, and you know I don't like that."

His reluctance would have been understandable if she knew the truth about his involvement in taking down the bad bear, but she didn't and couldn't. For Hap, this felt more like the beginning of the end instead of the new beginning he'd hoped for, but he knew she was right. The emotional baggage he had toted for years was not only heavy, but cumbersome. Though he'd never admit it to Weezie, he too had grown weary of the burden. Until closure with the Czar over Kate's death was behind him, Hap feared he might never move forward and reclaim complete sanity.

Knowing more than Hap did about stress disorder, Louise wasn't entirely sure he was fixable, but she wasn't about to give up trying. To do so, she was certain he first had to come to grips with his past, and then bury it for good if they were ever to have a future together. They had known each other since puberty, and though only becoming intimate in their twilight years, it was an enduring friendship that she was not about to abandon now.

After eating in near silence for what seemed an eternity, it was Weezie who spoke first, this time trying to begin anew with a fresh series of what should have been simple questions.

"So what's on that bucket list of yours now, how long is it, and are you getting near the end?"

"Truth is, it's getting longer and more challenging because I keep adding more things than I cross off."

"It really shouldn't be a competition, Hap."

"Well it is for me."

"You really like to win, don't ya?"

Given the alternative, that's a pretty safe bet."

"So losing isn't an acceptable outcome?"

"Never, and I'm not about to start now."

"How long has this been the case?"

"Probably since birth."

"That early?"

"I know you're looking for further evidence of some deep-seated root cause of my neuroses, so here's something you can psychoanalyze in your spare time. I've been determined from the very beginning. As legend has it, when I was all set to be born, my mother wasn't ready for delivery, so I just crawled outta there all by myself."

Once Weezie was done laughing, and with characteristic deadpan, Hap followed up with, "What's so funny? That's based on a true story my Dad used to tell, though it can't begin to touch the reason for Macbeth's fear of Macduff."

"Let's change gears, Hap. How about something less competitive, like your literary pursuits. Have you begun working on another bestseller?

"I'm always writing something and always have. Have you forgotten the veiled love notes that I sent you in junior high?"

"How could I, as they were thoughtful, honest, and tender. I remember marveling that as a teenager you could write with such remarkable poetic aplomb."

"I'm still at it, but hadn't ever planned on writing becoming the kind of pastime that would possess me."

"It should be a fun distraction, not a job. I mean, writing a book isn't like *real* work, right?

"Not if you find bleeding into a keyboard all fun and games."

"I'm sorry, I didn't mean it was easy. So what's left to write about?"

"As much as I've wanted to tell my own story, but have no aspirational desire for a Wikipedia page, I'm mulling over penning something that may bring some small measure of posthumous recognition."

"Pray tell, Hap – it'll be our little secret until it comes out in print long after we're gone."

"I want my extended family to know the real truth about my life, and I'm not leaving to chance how well or poorly my obituary will be written by some newspaper hack."

"It wouldn't surprise me if you'd already written it."

"Well…just a first draft."

"Ha! Let me guess – you were only able to stop after ten pages?"

"Actually twelve, but single-spaced."

Weezie laughed out loud, but all the while fearing what Hap revealed in jest might well be true. Morbidity wasn't his nature and was the last thing he should be thinking about before venturing off on a possibly ill-fated mission. Seeing this as an opportunity to steer the dialogue to where she might render some help, once the laughter stopped she continued.

"You know, before you turn taciturn and morose on me, maybe it's time for me to slip back into my ongoing role as your behavioral guru. God knows there's nobody else out there who has a decades-old baseline to measure the progression of your psychological disorders."

"Why not, and good segue, Doc. But only if you won't bill me for the analysis. Of course, I already know there'll be an upcharge for the emotional accompaniment."

"Do you ever run out of things to say?"

"So far, not yet, but do continue."

"Okay, here's the short version – you may not be ready to die, but maybe you're running out of reasons to live…and just so you know, I'm not gonna be the one who pushes you over the edge."

"My, you *do* know how to cut to the core, Dr. Porter. It's a wonder more of your patients aren't checking themselves into the loony bin *after* therapy. As for me, I'm just done trying to be relevant in today's age of craziness. Hell, I don't even know the new rules of engagement, let alone behavior. Maybe I've become no more than an anachronism with a heartbeat."

"Look Hap, maybe it's the scientist in me, but I know that as long as you have unfinished scores to settle, your excess baggage may be more than I bargained for."

"What scores?"

"Come on, your relentless pursuit of the one who could kill you, and I'd never recover from that."

"But I hear Moscow is beautiful this time of year and a place where I could find my own resurrection."

"Hap, you need to snap out of it. Instead of channeling *The Old Man and the Sea*, this time of your life should be more of a reflective Mister Rogers kind of moment for you."

"That's odd, as I knew Fred Rogers, who occasionally attended our church. In every conversation, he never failed to provide positive inspiration, but unlike you, he had a softer touch when doing so."

"With you I think the unvarnished truth works best, especially when up against someone whose recalcitrance is legendary."

"I can sit up and take the medicine, no matter how bitter, but what a shame Fred can't be here to reach out from the grave and help instead."

"Yeah, but given your host of issues, even he'd be stumped with a subject like you."

Weezie's comment allowed them both to relax a bit, which was sorely needed and a welcome relief. The remainder of the evening was civil, if not pleasant, and though their bodies may have ached for each other, neither of them made a move to pick up a room key when it was over. Not wanting it to end on such a sour note, Hap couldn't refrain from one more try.

"So Weeze, if I want a happy ending, the only way is to write it myself?"

"Since you're fond of talking yourself into most anything, I think that would be the best way, at least for now."

"Just remember, you'll never regret the things you've done as much as the things you didn't do."

"That's usually good advice, as I would expect from you, but not for tonight."

When they said their goodbyes in the parking lot, she kissed him, then said, "You know I love you, but won't share you with either a ghost or the demon who made her one."

"Kate's ghost will always be around to haunt me, but I plan to eliminate the demon who claimed her."

"I get that, but my fear for you is that defeating demons will only continue feeding your own."

It was common knowledge that spies came pre-wired with a default instinct for lying, whereas most others preferred telling the truth. Most everyone also knew that the worst and most damaging lies were the ones you told yourself. On his way back to Pittsburgh, Hap tried to convince himself that perhaps the ambiguous outcome of tonight's dinner with Weezie wasn't such a bad thing after all, but that too was a lie, and he knew it.

# CLEARED FOR DUTY

Having not heard from Bud in weeks, Hap was growing restless. Unwilling to be sidelined from any takedown of the Czar, he sensed it was time for another meeting with his one-time handler and now the country's chief spymaster. He didn't know how he would intercede – only that he must.

Somehow the Czar had managed to maintain his sordid tyrannical rule. His reign of terror was something the impoverished Russian people had grown accustomed to, but apparently not yet weary of. One reason was because his audacious strategies of testing the sovereignty of Russia's neighbors and one-time former satellites played well to a captive hometown audience. Much like the former American president, he had an uncanny ability to seize upon the worst of their innermost fears and exploit them under the cloak of nationalism.

Similarly, he exploited all there was to pillage from his fellow countrymen as the kleptocracy flourished. Estimates of the Czar's personal net worth ranged to four hundred billion dollars, or a third more than any other person on the planet. Of course, such information wasn't common knowledge among his own people. Nor were the nearly one hundred of his billionaire oligarchs that had been well fed from the Czar's table over the years. Any shred of optimism among the common folk had long been extinguished. There was no point in resisting what had become destitution for some and not much more than a bleak future for all others amid a country rife with corruption. Dissidents were routinely persecuted and prosecuted. Most perished after an abbreviated mock trial and jail sentence. Others simply vanished absent any evidence of arrest, conviction or imprisonment.

For all its supposed military might, the invasion of Ukraine revealed that Russia was relying on archaic Soviet-era weaponry and equipment to arm its assault. Following huge, unexpected troop losses, reluctant recruits were forcibly drafted, and after only a few days of training were sent to the front lines bearing rifles, thereby quickly becoming tank fodder for the Ukrainian army.

Given its vast size – eleven percent of the world's land mass, or twice the areas of either China or the United States, and despite its abundant natural resources, Russia was essentially on its way to ruin. The standard of living had improved in all the former satellites of the Soviet Union. However, in contrast, Mother Russia had stagnated while most of the wealth was skimmed off the top by the Czar and his cabal of thieves. America's gross domestic product of $24 trillion dwarfed Russia's $1.4 trillion, but even more revealing was that the USA's GDP per capita was $70,000 versus less than $10,000 for Russia.

With Ukraine, the Czar had woefully underestimated the intensity of the world's resolve and passion, betting instead on its ongoing complacency. Until now he had been left off the hook for all his atrocities since coming to power, but the world had changed and he hadn't. Despite leveling much of their country, he took a severe beating by the Ukrainians once they discovered the impotence of the Russian army. His battered ego drove him so far as to brandish the nuclear sword, but thankfully had replaced it in its scabbard.

The near global response to tyranny was both astonishing and, frankly, rational for a change. Given the world's resolve to survive, if not avoid direct conflict with Russia, it could not possibly have been otherwise. Nevertheless, with negotiations on everything with the civilized nations at a stalemate, worldwide paranoia of the Czar's next move continued unabated. By law, he had long ago extended his eligibility to continue ruling forever, which meant for life…or death.

It was no secret that Hap and plenty of others were hoping for the latter scenario, which was why he made an unscheduled visit to Langley. After being marshalled through the entire security protocol, he was escorted to the seventh floor and greeted by Bud's gatekeeper Patti.

"What mischief brings you in today, Hap? You must be up to no good."

"As usual, Patti, I'm always guilty of something."

"The boss doesn't always keep me in the loop, and apparently this is one of those times, so I'm guessing it must be yet another of your patriotic escapades."

"No, just a social call."

"Bullshit!"

"C'mon, Patti, you know how much he misses me."

"On some days that's true. Anyway, go on in, he's expecting you since being alerted of your arrival by security. Knowing how he hates to be caught off-guard, you really should have made an appointment."

"I like to surprise people; it gives me an edge and sometimes the upper hand."

"Just be forewarned that he appears more anxious today than usual."

Confirming Hap's expectations, Bud's office was a total mess. Unable to embrace the axiom that "cleanliness was next to Godliness", Bud welcomed the disarray and apparently could thrive only in such an environment. Hap was just the opposite, preferring orderliness all around him when working. Everyone knew the last thing Hap could ever be accused of was being haphazard.

Without looking up from his cluttered desk or offering any semblance of a greeting, Bud simply asked one of the questions that was always on his mind.

"So tell me, Hap, how's that private investment fund of yours doing?"

"Oh, you know, up about twice the S&P 500 so far, but the year isn't over and I expect it will outperform by an even wider margin."

"One of these days I'm hoping you'll let me in on some of that action."

"So Daddy still wants to get his beak wet, huh? Don't forget this little game of mine is really for enjoyment, and as I've told you before, occasionally there are losses."

"You don't mean like loss of *principal*?"

"Yeah, once in a blue moon, so it isn't like a CD. As I've told you before, Bud, investing is no longer my bread and butter. Nowadays I only do it for grins."

"I always wondered why you slick Wall Street gurus are always smiling."

"Those are the private equity and hedge fund boys who have to put their game faces on all the time; after all, for them, it *is* their daily bread. Just remember that mine is a hunch fund and *not* a hedge fund."

"What's the difference?"

"Actually, not much. Because I no longer have a dozen analysts on the payroll to vet my moves, now it's mostly all instinct."

"And what are you betting on now?"

"Same old formula, Bud – the stupidity and greed of others, but betting's not the right word – that's what idiots do on the outcome of a Steelers game, which for too many seasons now has been largely unpredictable."

"So if betting's not the right word, what is?"

"I suppose it's harnessing your conviction and courage based on actionable intel. Not much different than how decisions are made here at Langley. But remember, I don't dabble, so when I'm in, I'm *all* in by taking big positions."

"I'd never mistake you for a dabbler, Hap, but hope someday you'll deal me in on that game."

"We'll see, but only after we save the world so you can enjoy your retirement nest egg."

"Let's take a stroll, as I'll be needing some fresh air for what I expect you want to talk about."

Fresh air was Bud's euphemism for needing a cigarette or two along with a strong cup of coffee to fuel his brain with an overdose of stimulants. Taking a stroll was what many at Langley did when they needed to talk in private without fear of any eavesdropping. Once outside they found Bud's favorite bench empty; it was also strategically far removed from others who presumably were out and about for a similar experience.

"How soon do we rock and roll, Bud?"

"Well, so far, getting even tacit approval from on high has been the stumbling block. Given the Ukrainian situation, now POTUS welcomes opportunities to take private meetings with me, so I'm getting a lot better at reading him between the lines. In fact, though something like this could never be sanctioned at any level, I think he's very close to offering me an unspoken mandate to snuff the Czar."

That much was true, but Bud had to be careful, even with Hap, not to share everything he was privy to. There was universal agreement around the globe that an unchecked Czar was a cataclysmic threat to the future of humanity. Though never voiced aloud where they might be overheard or quoted, leaders of both the civilized and uncivilized world were joining the growing clarion call for his ouster or death. Bud and his colleagues were among the few who knew that the voice of POTUS in this unsung chorus was among the loudest.

"Bud, I don't know what the hell he's waiting for. Even if our role in this were ever discovered, the rest of the world would forgive us in a heartbeat."

"Maybe not everyone. Look, he's having a tough time justifying it, but will eventually come around."

"When he does, just remember that life's a one-way journey, so we'd better get it right the first time, especially with this slippery bastard. At best, we get one shot at this before the Czar is locked down and totally impregnable, so tell POTUS there's no time to be intellectually constipated."

"Relax, Hap; you're always in too big a hurry. Any hint of collusive action with the White House could be devastating, at least initially. While the president evaluates possible fallout and galvanizes support among all the key players, we just gotta sit tight and wait for his signal, no matter how subtle, before pulling any triggers. Of course, that doesn't mean we can't start planning. In fact, we already have a number of scenarios in play to do just that."

"Who's we?"

"Only the station chief – Sunny Day, and me."

Bud could read the skepticism on Hap's face, but wasn't prepared for his response.

"Since I'm obviously no longer among those in your inner orbit, what if I were off-book and had a little more free reign?"

"You don't get it, Hap. There are a few places in this world where you shouldn't go, and Russia's one of them. Moscow's no place for any of your cowboying behavior. They have their own rules of engagement over there, and if you don't follow them, you'll no longer be the predator, but the prey. I can get you in, but I can't get you out if you fuck up."

"That's not my style. Plus, with world opinion against him, the Czar has more to worry about than a solitary soldier like me looking to get even for something he's likely forgotten."

"Such vengeance could cloud your judgment when the time comes."

"I'd call it a reservoir of inspiration. Look, he's finally worried about his legacy. So far, his footnote in the history of the Slavic people would be presiding over the dismal decline, decay, and decadence of the once mighty Soviet Union. Even today the debris of communism remains scattered across most of Eastern Europe. Though his delusions about restoring its former territorial reach are irrational at best, just the fact that he believes he might pull it off is sobering and scary shit."

"But Hap, with nothing more to lose, this is the time we must keep his finger off the trigger of an apocalyptic nuclear showdown. He's finally understanding that Russia will forever be tarnished, much like the scourge of Hitler's permanent stain on Germany. Starting a war nobody wanted – even his own people – has catapulted him into second place behind only the Fuhrer for insanity. Nobody wants the last card he plays to be mutual annihilation, but it's possible."

"Which is precisely why now is no time for timidity."

As they strolled back to the building in silence, both were thinking about the similarities between the leaders of the Third Reich and the reformulated Russia. Both were madmen, tormented by their quest for greatness. They were unscrupulous, calculating, and yes, perhaps even part genius, but what they were not were men of faith and reason fashioned in God's image.

Apart from China and a few others, with the rest of the world united in combatting Kremlin aggression and its most recent reckless provocation, the hardship on the Russian people was now thrice as severe. Their growing unrest amid economic chaos was capable of bringing down the Czar, and he knew it, which was why he had become so ruthless. He imagined himself a monarch, all the while knowing his reign had no legitimacy.

Before reaching the building, and where their private conversation had to cease, Hap grabbed Bud by the shoulders and said, "Bud, I gotta be part of this and you know why."

"Okay, you will be, but not as a loose cannon. You may be meant to do this, but you'll have to be a lot more than self-anointed."

"Meaning what?"

"You'll have to abide by the rules."

"Whose rules?"

"Sunny Day, or Nikita, as she's now known over there in potato land."

"Nikita? As in Khrushchev? Isn't that a man's name?"

"Nope, it's both masculine and feminine, but given the scope of your last mission when partnered together, I'm betting she'll let you call her Nikki."

"What's her undercover last name?"

"I can only remember that it's hard to pronounce and am barely able to spell it without copying it from another document."

"That alone proves you've already passed by the off-ramp for retirement."

"Just remember, Hap, if you're cleared for this, I won't tolerate any hot-dogging; you gotta follow the rules while abiding by Sunny's orders. Right now she has a variety of possible plans, including yours, but none are definite or final yet. We get one shot at this and may never again get a second chance."

"You mean no improvisation if I feel her plan has to be amended?"

"Don't think I won't recall you at the first sign of insubordination."

"Don't worry, I'll be like Hannibal when attempting to lead the Carthaginian army across the Alps enroute to Rome and with some riding African elephants. As you may know, his answer to the troops' skepticism was, 'I will either find a way or make one.'"

"As usual, your confidence knows no bounds, so spare me the hype, Hap."

"I suppose the same goes for my occasional disobedience."

"And that's the problem. There was a time when I had high hopes of grooming you to be my successor. Hell, a former occupant of the White House and one of your staunchest supporters wanted to leap frog you right over me and into the Director's chair, but I convinced him you'd never agree."

"Apparently that president knew that those who can lead, lead, and those who can't, follow. Look, you know I'm not fond of sitting behind a desk, no matter how big. Plus, the politics and press briefings would be intolerable. Remember, Bud, this long-running position was always meant to be a side hustle for me."

"I know; plus, you're not always a team player. All you've ever wanted from this part time gig was to get the job done immediately and move on to the next assignment."

"Reminds me of another of my favorite pithy sayings, which is that the difficult work will be done immediately, whereas the impossible may take a little longer."

"Just remember that there's scant precedent for what we're about to do."

"C'mon, Bud, we've toppled regimes for decades, but I get it, we can't abide any sloppy work this time around."

"There's no margin for error, unless you want to spend the rest of your retirement years in a gulag."

"I don't think that's what the good Lord has planned for my ultimate calling."

"And Hap, what if you get caught over there? You know damn well we can't intervene."

"I'll figure something out."

"Not when finding yourself on center stage of an international incident like this one."

"This may surprise you, but when finding myself on center stage in the past, I discovered that I actually enjoy the spotlight."

"Nothing about you surprises me, Hap. Now, is there anything else you want from me?"

"Yes, but I'll wait for another day when you're in a better mood."

# PRIMING THE PUMP

CHRIS HAD BEEN THE IDEAL CANDIDATE and perfect recruit, but that didn't mean Hap had to like it. In most ways, he didn't, and had tried to prevent it. After all, Christian Franklin was his son. The deep-seated fear of a father for the safety of his child's life was not only understandable, but a natural, primal instinct. As his progenitor, Hap couldn't help but feel duty-bound to serve as Chris's protector as well.

Try as he did to hide the anxieties any parent would harbor, beneath all the apprehensions Hap was nevertheless secretly proud that Chris had chosen to serve his country in this dangerous way. Though at times worried that such thoughts might prove unforgivable, Hap's anxiety was overshadowed by the inner satisfaction he felt by his son's decision to follow the footpath of his father and grandfather. What set them apart had been Chris's recruitment itself. Whereas Hap and his father had been identified and sought by Langley, Chris had approached the CIA on his own.

Once Chris's initial application set off an avalanche of expected bells, whistles, and red flags, it was immediately referred to the DDO for special handling. Bud only smiled as he reviewed it because, unbeknownst to Hap, he had already started a file of his own on Chris. Beyond being someone whose special talents the agency desperately needed, Chris had the right DNA to fit right in. True to his calling as a master spy, Bud was skilled at keeping secrets, and knowing that Hap would go berserk if suspecting Langley might have Chris on its radar, that file had remained a very private one.

It was no wonder why Langley wanted Chris in its tent. His early pioneering work in artificial intelligence had placed him squarely in the NSA's gunsights a decade earlier, but all the agencies had been warned by the CIA that if it ever came to pass, Chris should rightly belong to them. Bud had to be patient, and he was, right up to the time when Chris's application and letter of inquiry arrived.

Inheriting his father's trader instinct, a year after Chris's start-up firm went public and its market cap exceeded a hundred million dollars, he was ready to cash in his chips and move on. To what, he wasn't sure, but Chris wanted it to be for something worth far more than money. He suspected what his father had long been doing for the flag, and it was more than an inkling. The clues were all there, and having assembled all the misshapen pieces of the puzzle, Chris's analytical mind could now see the entire picture, which only served to heighten his curiosity about the covert dimension of Hap's life.

For obvious reasons, Bud himself had taken the first interview with Chris. They warmed to each other from the start, and to Bud, it was not much different than when he had recruited Hap decades earlier. Both were affable, smart, sharp-witted and suffered no fools. His only concern was that Chris might prove as hard to manage as Hap had been.

Since the Cold War, three generations had been fed a steady diet of books, movies, and television series that glamorized undercover operatives, especially the ones with licensure to kill with impunity. Hollywood knew what sold, so it wasn't surprising that the studios continued feeding the public hunger and insatiable thirst for more of it. Despite the dichotomy of his public and private lives, Hap recognized the importance of remaining detached from the mythology portrayed on the silver screen. In fact, Hap had once told Bud that he likened much of the available weaponry in his tool kit to what women considered girdles and pantyhose to be – necessary evils, but nonetheless all instruments of the Devil.

Once the bloom was off the rose, Hap's work at Langley became like any other job. He got up, grabbed a coffee, saluted the flag and went to work. Like his best counterparts at the Mossad, MI6, or even the FSB, there was little difference in their approach to the daily grind than that of any other working stiff. For most others who toiled as spies, the fascination never wore off, and the tradecraft was alluring for all the wrong reasons. Thankfully, it was clear to Bud that Chris wouldn't end up being one of that kind. Instead, like his father, Chris viewed serving the country as simply payback for the good fortune of a privileged life full of countless blessings.

When Bud could no longer afford to keep the secret, he called Hap on a secure line to report the latest update on Chris. His motivation included not wanting Hap to find this out from Chris directly before Bud could begin shaping the narrative. Hap's reaction was predictable.

"Bud, I thought we'd been through this – two generations of Franklins is all you get, so it's gotta stop now."

"Remember Hap, as you well know, it was *we* who found you, but it was *he* who found us. I wasn't out there trolling for your son."

"But Chris doesn't have a dog in this fight; only I do."

"And yours is a pit bull. Look, we all have dogs in this fight, but only a very few have the right breed to succeed, and from my perspective, Chris's is one of them."

"And how will you keep him out of harm's way?"

"We've set Chris up in California with his own remote computer lab and an unlimited budget. He's already up and running with astonishing success. If need be, we can always bring him in after an operation goes down. For now, he's where he needs to be and where he's most useful. In fact, he's happy figuring out bad shit and writing code to combat it."

"Of all people, Bud, you should know that recognizing the aroma of danger is a well-developed and innately human trait that can't be replicated by an algorithm."

"I think you're just afraid and maybe a little jealous that a former grandmaster of computer gaming might control the world's destiny."

Bud was right. Evolution of the dark arts was inevitable, and there was no point for Hap to stand in the way. Technologically talented folks like Chris were the new kids on the block; they could and would take the cloak and dagger business to a new level. And despite knowing so much about how the world worked, relics like Hap and Bud would soon be forced onto the sidelines to make room for the new generation.

Though effective in their day, methods of espionage used by Hap and his father before him hadn't changed much. But nowadays, taking the bad guys out one at a time was becoming old school. The firepower of Chris's keyboard was equally lethal and could replace all the conventional armaments Hap and other aging agents packed in their Go Bags. Even taking outdoor "strolls" with Bud would no longer be needed when replaced by reliably encrypted video chats.

One missing element from such a new paradigm was improvisation, which had been something Hap excelled at. Sure, artificial intelligence was heady stuff, but to his knowledge, computers could not yet react spontaneously to any unpredicted elements of a mission. Hap was pretty sure that capability could only be processed by the brain of a seasoned operative.

"There's something else you should know, Hap."

"If I should, then I must, so go right ahead and illuminate me."

"You remember Paradiso?"

"How could I forget."

Paradiso was the name given by Dmitri Cherkov to the Caribbean island where he had set up an elaborate computer apparatus devoted to rampant cybercriminality of all kinds. For a time, Paradiso had been the foremost state-sponsored hacker in the world. Its sophisticated data-mining software had succeeded in draining bank accounts, upsetting power grids, penetrating systems to steal industrial secrets, and planting disruptive malware.

Initially, Cherkov's intentions for Paradiso were limited to pirating in cyberspace. However, beyond the outright looting and industrial espionage, the Czar's primary interest was in weaponizing his favorite oligarch's troll farm for something else – spreading all manner of blatant falsehoods to erode the faith of the western world in its democracies. Such a sustained campaign of disinformation was nothing short of waging ideological warfare.

Once discovered by Hap and the CIA, Cherkov's entire complex was dismantled and shipped by the Navy to California for reassembly stateside. The thinking was that it could be repurposed and turned against Russia and China in similar fashion while also serving as a purveyor of unfiltered and unbiased news to sow unrest and undermine communism. As with the defense contractors, the CIA had longstanding special relationships with the companies that had given Silicon Valley its name. When given the opportunity to examine the guts of Cherkov's cutting edge troll farm, they all were delighted to comply when Washington asked to requisition some of their top wizards.

"And Hap, think about the odds of our shipping all that computer shit we confiscated from Cherkov to a base near Chris so he'd have easy access to it. How convenient!"

"Which base, Bud? There are 32 military bases in California representing all branches of the armed forces."

"What's the difference. Take your pick, but the location is so classified that I can't tell you or even confirm it if you guess."

"So my son knows but I can't! Who do you think risked his fuckin' life so Uncle Sam could get his hands on that stuff?"

"That doesn't really matter now. What does is that Chris has been busy harvesting some of Paradiso's capabilities to help him cripple what needs to go silent in Moscow when you make your move on the Bear."

"Fine, but one more thing, Bud."

"Go ahead, what now? I'm just sitting here on a pincushion full of sharp needles waiting for the next gumshoe to drop."

"I want to visit Chris before this thing gets too far ahead of us, and I'll need a fast plane to get me there and back in a day."

"God almighty, you're already testing me with your freelancing."

"You owe me that and so much more."

"Still keeping score, are you?"

"Just charge it against the hundreds of millions we confiscated from Cherkov when taking him down."

"Fine, but to and from San Jose will require two different pilots due to the inflight time restrictions."

"Understandably so, but I didn't make the rules. Just make sure you requisition a quiet bird with a fully reclining seat or private berth so I can sleep both ways. Oh, and as a heads up, I can be free to go in the morning."

"But if you insist on going tomorrow, I may have to borrow something like that from the Air Force, and those bastards hate mustering an asset on such short notice."

"I'm not looking for a two-seater F-16B, though that would be faster than what they'll send for a low life spy. Besides, I know you exchange expensive gifts with the armed forces all the time and occasionally let them play with our toys too, so just make it happen. I'm sure you have some spare bargaining chips stashed away for just such a favor."

"I got a whole drawer full of them, but I'm hanging up on you now before you demand anything else."

"You mean like a private car and driver to get me safely to Christian's home? That'd be nice, Bud. After all, you know how I hate navigating all that slow traffic on the congested highways the Californians somehow seem to tolerate."

"Say goodbye, Hap."

# THE BIG REVEAL

T HE SOBERING SPECTER of another Franklin joining the dark side was almost unendurable. After careful consideration of how he might approach Chris, Hap proceeded to do so in his typical manner, which was simply to confront him. He did so by surprising Chris on his home turf in California. Silicon Valley was a place Hap had rarely visited and for good reason. He was convinced that the cradle of electronic wizardry represented what robbed humanity of engaging and exercising the brain when in search of a solution. Instead, the search engines born and managed from there were permitted to puke up anything and everything with no regard to its veracity. But Hap's overriding fear was precisely what his son had made a fortune doing – fast-tracking nature through artificial intelligence and building autonomous systems with very little human oversight. Despite his reservations, Hap knew it was time to put America back to work by resurrecting Yankee ingenuity and know-how before China further tightened its stranglehold on the West.

Chris was indeed caught off-guard when Hap presented himself at the doorstep unannounced, but that didn't mean he was unprepared for what he knew was next. He had been expecting the confrontation and dreaded it might end up being an unpleasant showdown with his father. It didn't take long. After the obligatory small talk and a tall drink to bolster his resolve, Hap began the inquisition.

"Have you seriously considered what you're getting yourself into?"

"Why, Dad, whatever do you mean by that?"

"You know damn well, and you might have talked to me before Bud Smith."

"Oh rats, so he ratted me out, huh? That's hardly the thing good spooks are known for."

"Just so you know, Chris, some spies can't keep secrets."

"Wait! What? So you're one of them?"

"Did Bud tell you that?"

"No, but you just confirmed it, and for the record, it's not so stunning a revelation. I've always suspected something like this was in your skill set but missing from your official resumé."

"So the cat's outta the bag, huh? Just promise me one thing – let's keep this between us; your sister doesn't need to know any of it."

"Yeah, Lindsay's got more than enough on her plate to worry about."

"The brain comes pre-wired for what you need in life, Chris, but I'm afraid Lindsay's has become overloaded because painful thoughts are now crowding out the pleasurable ones. Maybe someday you and your techie compadres can come up with a way to offload her unnecessary worries onto an external hard drive and then recycle it the old-fashioned way – in a dumpster."

"That only happens with artificial intelligence when we can program the deletion of things that are unnecessarily frightening. Human intelligence may want to dismiss the bad and damaging elements, but can't, so maybe God wants it to remain there and knows that maybe one day it will be helpful instead of harmful."

"Good answer, son, but creating this artificial intelligence without a conscience sounds more akin to jump-starting evolution through genetic engineering. How do you govern the intentionality of an AI directive made without a moral compass, common sense, and loads of experience? Anyway, this is getting way beyond the boundaries of my intellectual capacity."

"But not your curiosity, right Dad?"

"No, but you can enlighten me another day. Before we go off on another tangent, let's get back to the real purpose of this little *tête-à-tête*."

"Single-minded and riveted as always, but okay, I can tolerate another of your endurance tests a while longer."

"Look Chris, you know I love you, so just trust me on this. Once you get mixed up with Langley there's no way out. It's inescapable, and you can't begin to comprehend the risks of your involvement. You've always had good judgment, so use some of it now before it's too late."

"You don't trust me to make my own decisions independently? You know, Dad, you didn't teach me *everything* I know."

"That's obvious, but we all can use a little mentoring from time to time."

"Bud sees my involvement as being peripheral to where the action occurs and damage is done, so I don't see myself in any jeopardy."

"You can't hide from the danger; sooner or later it'll find and ensnare you."

"The only danger is when we deploy troops, and why would we do that? Future wars will be waged in outer space where the only collateral damage will be limited to the debris of space junk eventually falling from orbit."

"Chris, that's a long way off; today's warfare is still fought right here on Mother Earth."

"But with lotsa help by counterintelligence initiatives through global electronic eavesdropping, deciphering encrypted data, digital scrambling, and jamming navigational signals. The networks that now manage the world all rely on technology. And guess what, all those networks have exploitable security flaws."

"So where do you fit in?"

"For starters, cyberespionage, or the collection and corruption of data, is the new frontier, and it's all discoverable. Cryptography has come a long way since Thomas Jefferson's cipher wheel, and yes, before you remind me, I know he was, and still is, America's only Renaissance Man."

"See, you *did* learn something from me after all. I'm also well aware of the developments to Mr. Jefferson's wheel, including when Station X in Bletchley Park outside London broke the ciphers of Nazi Germany's enigma machine during the war."

"That's ancient history, Dad. All information is perishable, and that's true in both of your worlds – Wall Street and whatever you do in the name of national security."

"Information only begets knowledge, but experience can bring wisdom. If you're paying attention so far, then you'll get my point."

"Which is?"

"Wisdom is what you bring to knowledge."

"Wisdom for enlightened decision-making today depends more on next generation quantum computing than one's memory."

"Which really means AI technologies communicating directly with each other, and worse yet, maybe collaborating without the wisdom of human oversight or intervention."

"That's the plan, Dad."

"But you can't program morality."

"Not entirely, but we're getting close."

"Bull shit. Differentiating right from wrong or distinguishing love from hate is only discernible by an experienced, adaptive brain."

"And we're trying to replicate that very thing."

"Then, as in *Titus Andronicus*, feel free to cut off and bake my head in a pie – it's all yours."

"And then what?"

"Though not available in Shakespeare's day, the next step should be obvious – just clone what's inside."

"No thanks; like others of your ilk, it would be a flawed specimen. I'm pretty sure you've got a lotta outdated software still running up there."

"Maybe so, but I was thinking more about the potential value of the outrageously high personal tax deduction I could take for such a gift to modern science."

After sharing a good laugh, Chris stared lovingly at Hap, trying to absorb all that his father meant to him, then said, "It's time for *you* to trust *me*, Dad, and especially on this one. Just keep the faith."

"So you've accepted the position?"

"I have, and some time ago, but I suspect you already knew that."

"Actually I didn't, or I would have been here long before now."

"And just so there are no more surprises, we'll be working in tandem on this Russian caper, though I don't have any of the details yet beyond your involvement."

"And let me guess, all this hinges on your renowned specialty – artificial intelligence. If so, give me a practical example of how that impacts outright conventional warfare."

"I can develop and run a series of situational analyses that can predict a given enemy's behavior and its next likely strategic battlefield move."

"And unlike in a chess game, this happens in what – nanoseconds?"

"Exactly, and hallelujah, Dad, as there may be hope for you yet."

"Don't forget I've lived through a technological tidal wave, whereas you came along well after the world changed for folks like me who find it impossible to stay relevant."

"I could help you with that, but it'd be a long, challenging tutorial that you couldn't, or wouldn't, stay awake for."

"I have a better idea. Why don't I just do my thing the old way while you keep a close eye on me from your widescreen monitor here in La-La Land."

"I'm not sure I could be that vigilant if you go off the reservation and get reckless."

"It's worked for me in the past."

"Yeah, maybe so, but this here's an entirely new game for a resistant old-timer like you."

"I'm proud to have been raised in the Jurassic Period when we learned good manners. We even had a book to rely on called *Miss Manners*, which I'm certain neither you nor Lindsay ever read."

"How can you be so sure?"

"Because, as always, your impudence and insubordination never fail to disappoint."

"Wonder where I got that…certainly not from Mom."

"You got her patience."

"And she needed lots of that because it was one of several virtues you didn't get."

"Chris, I may have been short-changed on some, but always try to make up for the shortcomings with other qualities where I got full helpings."

"In some cases, probably more than a belly full. Maybe it's time you learned that being overcompensated can be much like an overdose."

"There you go again, disrespecting your elders. Well, if I can't change your mind, let me welcome you to the family business, or at least one of them. It's something my own father never had the chance to do with me."

"Hold on, are you saying I'm a *third* generation legacy?"

"I'm not saying anything. You're now on a need-to-know basis, and right now you don't need to know any more about that. Trust me, son, it's better you remain in the dark, so just give me a hug and we'll call it even."

"Okay Dad, but where's your luggage?"

"Didn't need any; I'm flying back today."

"Really? Why?"

"Because there's a very expensive private bird standing by at the airport, and I've got things to do at home."

"Like what?"

"Things I can't talk about."

"Can't or won't?"

"Both."

"Before you go, Dad, I should probably thank you, as this went better than I ever could have imagined."

"That's only because I was biting my tongue the whole time."

"Baby steps indeed, but progress nonetheless."

# SPARTACUS REVISITED

ESPITE BEING DESPERATELY IN NEED OF IT, HAP couldn't sleep a wink on the return flight to Pittsburgh. Confirming Christian's involvement brought a new dimension to operation *Bad Bear Down*, and Hap was conflicted. While duty-bound to complete the assignment, he was hesitant to do so when it might put his son at risk if he failed. He hadn't had much experience with failure and didn't want this time to be its introduction.

There was no doubt the Czar had it coming to him for a host of blatant assaults against humanity. Short of a long public crucifixion, there was no penalty severe enough for the war crimes and other atrocities he'd committed. Beyond the most egregious sins were orchestrating political interference in democracies, crypto heists, raking in enormous proceeds from illicit transactions through private blockchain networks, and arming virtually any renegade regime seeking to undermine the West.

Hap, of course, wanted the Czar's demise to be excruciatingly painful for his own personal reasons. When musing about it, several came to mind. His favorite was to saddle a horse, and after tying a rope around the Czar's ankles, drag him for a mile or so through rough, rocky terrain covered in thorny sagebrush. Then, like the gripping scene from the movie *Spartacus*, an additional improvisation might include strapping the Czar's near-lifeless body or severed head to a spike for all the world to witness. Though knowing such a gory public display could never happen, Hap enjoyed ruminating about it privately.

Langley had toyed with other ideas, including the Czar's own signature toxin. The Russian nerve agent novichok would be a perverse ending for a man who had used it to silence dissidents and political rivals like Alexei Navalny. But that wasn't the kind of payback Hap sought. He wanted it to be personal, and to do so meant delivering the final death blow himself and at close range. Taking such a risk, of course, might jeopardize Hap's children if things went badly.

As with most covert missions, information would be separated into silos, with only those in command having access to all the moving parts. This meant that few, if any, beyond Bud could see the whole chessboard. It would start with a blanket power outage. For Christian, defeating the electrical grid and jamming cell phone networks would be child's play. Pandemonium would ensue, but the bedlam might only be temporary, as there was no way to determine if and how long it might take the Russkies to repair the interference.

Unaccustomed to, and unprepared for, an outside assault on the seemingly impenetrable Russian infrastructure would enrage the Czar. Beyond the havoc created and initial embarrassment, it would also prove difficult to assemble all the needed moving pieces to work in harmony to restore order. Getting Hap close to the Czar was Sunny's assignment, but he would not be briefed on those details until arriving in Moscow. How long Hap might have to finish the job was anybody's guess, and he knew it.

Apart from the unknown variables, Hap thought the plan was as good as any. The weakest link would be the discovery of him as an unwelcome intruder. He worried that the biggest impediment was that he didn't speak or understand much Russian. Though conversant in French and Spanish, Hap's command of other foreign languages was limited. He had an aptitude for dialect and could make one sound like the other, but despite recent efforts to bone-up on his Russian with a crash course, Hap was all but certain he couldn't fool an FSB agent. At the very least, once in Moscow he would have Sunny engage him in dialogue every day until the time came.

# FUELING THE RAGE

**F**OR THIS ASSIGNMENT, Hap needed no motivation beyond the obvious. His wrath had been simmering for years over the hit on Kate, so he had more skin in the game than the others involved in *Bad Bear Down*. Although their collective malice wouldn't be expected to approach his own personal inducement, Hap expected all team players to step up in a big way.

Of course, public outrage wasn't limited to just the Czar. The world was literally falling apart, and what God had carefully and lovingly created, too many others seemed hell-bent on putting asunder. It was time the Czar and others like him on the global stage were put down for good, and that alone should provide the satisfaction they sought.

Hap had a lingering reservation about the transportation aspect, as that was one dimension of the plan that could run afoul and screw up the entire operation before it was set in motion. Getting into and out of a foreign country often posed more of a danger than executing the mission itself, and this time it would be Mother Russia itself, where the barriers to entry were monumental.

If caught, punishment would be unmerciful. The last time Hap had been held prisoner by a Russian was no picnic, but a living horror. His captor and interrogator was none other than his longtime nemesis, Dmitri Cherkov. At the time, Cherkov was the favored oligarch and former fellow KGB colleague of the Czar. The torture Hap endured in a Brussels bunker had included all manner of bizarre rituals courtesy of Cherkov's sadistic genius and fondness for barbarity.

One of the most debilitating had been something called Piñata, but it was not the festive version children played at birthday parties. Rather, it was the most brutal savagery Hap could have imagined. First, his head was covered by something that resembled a football helmet, but with only two peepholes for his eyes. Hap soon learned that was to make sure he would see what was coming next. Once chained by his ankles and suspended upside down about six feet from the floor, the game began with his captors putting on blindfolds and taking turns at him with baseball bats for Cherkov's amusement. The initial strike felt like he had been shot in the head by a cannon ball. Others missed their intended target and landed on his shoulders and torso. After a dozen or so blows that hit their mark, the helmet cracked, Hap lost consciousness, and the barbaric beating stopped.

Though the headache that followed was a real doozy, Hap had survived the traumatic ordeal, but only after following an extended concussion protocol and convalescence. Years later the entire story and lurid details of his captivity would be well-chronicled elsewhere, but the short version was that Cherkov was brought to justice, or at least that's what the CIA had intended. Instead, however, the oligarch eventually was traded away for Weezie in a high stakes prisoner exchange.

It had all begun two years earlier when the celebrated Dr. Louise Porter was scheduled to speak at an international symposium in Brussels, where she was abducted by Cherkov and used as bait to summon Hap's predictable attempt to rescue her. Hap was Cherkov's real target, and once captured, was imprisoned and interrogated. Forever scorched into his optic nerve, Hap's recall of his gruesome treatment and the protracted series of events that followed would never be forgotten and remained a source of vivid nightmares.

Fortunately, once the tables were turned and Cherkov became the CIA's prisoner, the Czar's own FSB agents stepped in and took Weezie hostage in order to get their own man back in a trade. Brokered directly with the Czar, the State Department and all others involved in the swap believed that would be the end of Cherkov. Most assumed that when he arrived back on Russian soil, the Czar would do away with him, but that was not to be.

Upon his return to Moscow, instead of being summarily executed, Cherkov's life was spared. Initially, he was left to rot in solitary confinement for nearly a year until the Czar had use for him. Cherkov's transition began with restoration of his health. Severed by Hap with an axe in Brussels, Cherkov's missing right hand was replaced with a bionic version that possessed uncommon strength, even if a bit short on dexterity. He never quite mastered the transition to being left-handed, including using it when on the toilet or during lonely nights trying to affirm the aptronym of his last name. In return for such rehabilitation and clemency, Dmitri Cherkov was only too eager to reaffirm his fealty to the Czar.

It took a few years of hard and nasty work to resurrect his arms-trafficking empire, but with Kremlin support, Cherkov returned to his former position of prominence and power. Despite his success and abundant wealth, it was only his boundless ego that went missing after it had been all but stripped away by Hap and then the Czar. Cherkov's longing for immediate and permanent gratification was  precisely the kind of frailty that could befall him once again. The CIA suspected this and had acted upon it, setting in motion a scenario to encourage Cherkov's ultimate betrayal of his patron Czar. Though Hap didn't know it yet, he was about to find out from Bud that it was none other than Sunny Day who had orchestrated the defection.

# FINAL PETITION

LUCKILY, THE PLANS FOR *Bad Bear Down* were not yet final and remained on the drawing board at Langley. As was typical, Hap had some modifications in mind, and in a departure from standard protocol, would take his suggestions directly to the top as always.

This time the meeting with Bud Smith was a scheduled one. Even Patti's greeting upon Hap's arrival signaled that they were expecting him to play nice for a change.

"So, Hap, you decided to call ahead and book an appointment like everyone else. You know, the boss actually likes that. Some might call it common courtesy."

"Don't be surprised; you know I'm capable of following the rules just like regular people."

"Hogwash! Now get in there before he changes his mind about seeing you. You're supposed to be reporting to someone a little lower on the food chain on this one, Hap, and not the Boss Man himself."

"How'd you know that?"

"I keep my eyes and ears open."

"Then I bet you'd be good at undercover work."

"All kinds, Hap, all kinds; if you only knew."

"But what about keeping quiet about it?"

"During or after? Now that wouldn't be any fun, would it? But do keep it up, Hap – the banter, I mean."

"At my age, that may be the only thing I can."

As usual, Bud's thunderous voice saved Hap and Patti from getting too close to the edge of reality.

"If you're done out there, get in here before I turn you away on principle."

"But Bud, you don't have any principles."

"They were checked at the door of this place 40 years ago. Don't make yourself comfortable, Hap, we're gonna take a little stroll."

"You got it bad, don't you, Bud?"

Hap knew that what Bud meant by a stroll was that he needed a cigarette as much as the privacy an outside walk would provide. Bud pulled on his badly wrinkled suit coat, grabbed his cigarettes and well-worn vintage Zippo lighter from his desk, and took Hap by the arm as they exited.

Once seated on what everyone knew was the DDO's personal bench and outdoor smoking parlor, Bud began with an update on the mission planning by revealing some, but not all, of the ideas that had been percolating. He also advised Hap that they could no longer be seen together and that his assistant director for operations would be taking over if the mission was approved. Given the absence of any heated blowback from Hap, who had long been accustomed to reporting only to the DDO, Bud felt it was safe to drop what he knew would be the ultimate bombshell.

"The real shocker might as well come from me as well, Hap, so brace yourself. We've recruited Dmitri Cherkov's assistance in getting you into the country."

"No fucking way. We can't trust that bastard, particularly with me in the wind over there. Since when did we become that desperate?"

"Hear me out first. He's had a conversion of sorts, and yes, though somewhat driven by greed, it's really his ego that he'd rather have stroked. He's precisely the one we want running things over there once we remove the problem."

"If true, that would rival the conversion of Saul to Saint Paul, and you know it. He's no more than a left-handed wanker."

"Maybe, but we need a tough guy near the top who could offer a clear path forward from the growing civil unrest. Sure, his businesses would thrive when no longer under the heavy thumb of the Czar, but eventually he could bring reform and has a chance to force the other oligarchs to get in line and do the same. They know it's the only way out for them in order to enjoy what they've already plundered and gotten away with so far."

"That's a long shot, Bud, and how can you be so sure? I've seen his true colors up close, and in case you've forgotten, he's the guy who almost beat my brains out. So who's the go-between?"

"He cleverly initiated contact with the Moscow station during the run-up to the Ukraine invasion. As you yourself might have experienced, Sunny Day is very good at sensing vulnerability, particularly in men."

"No comment."

"By appealing to his vanity, she gained his confidence over time, only to discover that he *really* believes he could re-shape Russia for the good. Maybe with age comes wisdom, and Sunny's convinced Cherkov would like not only to be revered during his lifetime, but remembered for all time."

"Oh spare me the fairy tale; a vicious tiger like him doesn't simply lose his stripes overnight. Profits and pleasures are his only motivators."

"Remember, Hap, he first tasted the freedoms of America first-hand when married to Dr. Porter. Secondly, his brethren kingpins that control the entire economy now spend most of their time on foreign soil, and there's an unspoken reason for that."

"What's that?"

"Oh c'mon, it's freedom. We need Cherkov and the others to help in a transition to democratic rule. Without our presence and influence, Russia could fall apart; life there doesn't stop – that would be like Afghanistan."

"You're saying a little corruption could be tolerated to prevent a reversion to mayhem?"

"Actually, Hap, a little corruption will sustain it until reform happens."

"And what if his conversion isn't genuine?"

"We have ways to keep him under the hammer if it gets to that. Though you weren't privy to how easily he caved under interrogation the last time we had him in custody, he spilled the beans on Poppa Bear right in front of the camera. He knows that releasing that footage would bring a swift slash to his throat from a sharp sickle."

"So how is he helping us get to the Czar?"

"From the sidelines only, and it'll be mostly you he's helping. Like many of the others close to the Kremlin, some of his extravagant play toys have been seized under sanction, including a $350 million custom Boeing 787 Dreamliner."

"And let me guess, we're gonna give it back to him?"

"Actually, we're even going to deliver the bird by flying it back to his estate outside Moscow where he has his own 10,000 foot state-of-the-art private runway."

"Why that long, takeoff only requires 8,000 feet at most?"

"Who the hell knows, but he's overly cautious when it comes to his own safety these days. Maybe he's worried his pilots might miss the touch down mark and overshoot it. But here's the exciting part – you'll be on that flight as its sole pampered passenger."

"You're kidding me."

"It's the best and safest way in, as nobody bothers to check the flights of the oligarchs when they land on private airstrips. Unless, of course, you're fond of skydiving and want to parachute in from some fuckin' place like Belarus and hitchhike your way to Moscow. If not, then this is the current plan."

"And who's in the cockpit?"

"Cherkov's chief pilot in the left seat and one of ours in the right. You'll be posing as the third pilot when embarking and deplaning, but won't be anywhere near the flight deck when in the air."

"How about extraction? That'll be more difficult; it always is."

"Same way."

"That may be more problematic once the bedlam begins. No matter who ends up being in charge, I'd think they'd move to high alert and ground all outbound flights. Who's our Yankee co-pilot?"

"Not sure yet, but it'll have to be a subcontractor. As you know, all operational details have to be compartmentalized for security reasons, especially in this case. All will be revealed, but not until showtime."

"But your subcontractors are all mercenaries who got their wings courtesy of Uncle Sam in Iran and Afghanistan. Not unlike the Vietnam veterans, too many of your recent recruits are fucked-up with PTSD."

"Actually not that many, but I'm told a lot of them do smoke a little weed to settle their nerves before takeoff."

"Get with it, Bud – weed, or the Devil's cabbage, is now called cannabis and no longer smoked. These days they bake it into a tasty Rice Krispies loaf and eat it, which is why they're called edibles."

"Where *do* you learn this shit, Hap, the internet?"

"Never googled a damned thing in my life, Bud – I only read hardback books and printed newspapers."

"Ignorance must be blissful, Hap."

"Anyway, if this thing goes in the crapper, I want my own guy to swoop in and fish me out."

"I get it now. You want me to recall your friend, Mac, out from retirement?"

"Well yeah, because he's someone who won't shit his pants at the first sign of trouble. Apart from being an improvisor like me, Mac's a battle-tested experienced aviator who can ignore the onboard computer and fly by the seat of his pants with nothing more than intuition and a steady hand on the joystick."

"I figured you'd pull something like this, so I've already checked up on him. By the way, and maybe you don't know this, but beyond being your childhood friend and flying the corporate jet at Sterling Capital after his retirement, he's done a few side jobs for us over the years."

"Really? No, I wasn't aware of that, but Mac's tight-lipped, which is another reason he'd be my choice."

"But he hasn't maintained his certification since leaving American Airlines, and might be a bit rusty after being holed-up at his remote castle on the lake since before the pandemic."

"I'm sure you know he's flown everything shy of the space shuttle. It's in his blood. Why, he occasionally still wears his father's bomber jacket from World War II. As for prying him loose from his comfy hammock, I'll get him onboard with this; he's probably lonely and needs the action."

"You'll do no such thing. I'll reach out to him myself and make an assessment. If it's a go, I'll let you know, but you are forbidden to have any direct contact. According to his file, Mac's only commanded a 777, so to get up to speed he'll need a few days in Seattle inside a Boeing flight simulator for transitioning to the newer 787 model. Besides, we're adding a few new bells and secret whistles to Cherkov's plane that he'll have to master, but that's something else you don't need to know about now. Just know the bird will be equipped with everything we've got."

Cherkov's luxury airliner had been hidden in a top secret hanger at one of the former British RAF bases not far from London and now run by the United States. At considerable taxpayer expense, but well disguised within the defense budget, the plane was being temporarily retrofitted with the latest stealth and evasive maneuvering technology. Such upgrades resulted from an unlikely collaboration between the leading aerospace defense contractors, which were typically fierce competitors for pieces of the Pentagon's pie and whose proprietary work was otherwise shrouded in secrecy.

Making this happen was due to the ongoing cozy relationship between top brass at the Defense Department and the most senior executives at companies like Lockheed Martin, General Dynamics, Raytheon and Boeing. It was no secret that the Defense Department knew in advance which company would be awarded certain contracts long before the sealed bids were opened. The process was more like a game of round robin, designed to make certain all of the players' plates were full while guaranteeing the practice wouldn't unravel. Though leery of working alongside the others, contractors always fell into line to secure their places at the feed trough of Uncle Sam's gravy train.

If and when the newly laden jetliner ever returned from Russia, all the special gear would be stripped and dismantled without a trace before the aircraft would be turned over to its owner as agreed. Unlike some other federal agencies, the CIA always kept its word when bargaining for help, and Cherkov knew he could count on that agreement.

Over the years Hap had learned to trust Bud, who had become close to a father figure. He also knew that embellishing the truth when necessary had become an art form for the DDO. Though somewhat skeptical, this time Hap would have to trust that Bud would do his best to recruit Mac. For him it wouldn't necessarily be a deal breaker if Mac were not on the team, but he also knew Bud didn't enjoy being threatened. Beyond Mac's competency, what Hap really sought and needed this time was the self-assurance that all would go well. Only the best of friends could do that, and they were hard to find. Over the years, finding ones that Hap could put up with and who could put up with him wasn't that easy. Mac was one of those.

# THAT'S NO WAY TO SAY GOODBYE

Besotted with her for nearly a lifetime, it was only natural that Hap needed to see Weezie before his life might end. The truth was that although desperate for some closure with her before leaving for Russia, he probably knew from the start it was not to be. That didn't stop him from calling her.

"Weeze, can you come for the weekend?"

"That depends on what you have planned."

"I was thinking we might work in the yard and then till the garden."

"I bet you were."

"At my place weeding is a non-stop event, and absent any spectators, it's a fairly lonely chore."

"You'd better get used to being lonely, Hap. How are things in Fox Chapel? Some days I miss it."

"Bucolic as ever, but it's harder and harder to keep the riffraff out."

"You mean burglars?"

"No, some of the new residents."

"Since when did you become an elitist?"

"The conversion didn't happen overnight, but only after aging and lotsa reflection."

Weezie knew Hap's claim was a blatant falsehood, as they both were made from the same social fabric. Excepting the snobby, snooty nouveau riche that had flocked there since, the Borough of Fox Chapel that Hap and Weezie knew as youngsters really wasn't so different now.

Unspoiled for centuries while occupied by Native Americans, its pristine forests were first invaded by well-heeled captains of industry during the early 1900s as a pastoral refuge from the growing city of Pittsburgh. Urban exodus wasn't uncommon in the other large metropolitan areas that had built America, but rather a logical extension of growing prosperity.

Migration to Pittsburgh's suburbs accelerated after the Second World War, but due to foresight, thoughtful planning and minimum-acreage zoning restrictions, Fox Chapel was spared from being overbuilt like most other bedroom communities. The end result was that it attracted only newcomers of privilege. Such an axiom was true in other instances, as virtually anything deemed exclusionary was coveted all the more. After all, everyone knew that pretty much everything in life but God's love was rationed by price.

A handful of scions remained from "the Borough's" earliest settlers. Their ancestors' estates once comprised vast tracts of land, which was the one thing the Lord wasn't making any more of. But when the third or fourth generational trust funds eventually began drying up, these descendants of the industrial revolution's titans resorted to selling off portions of their families' Fox Chapel real estate holdings. Such sales of their heritage typically weren't by choice, but by necessity in order to extend their lazy, lavish lifestyles yet a little longer before the inevitable shit hit the fan and they were reduced to paupers.

Inherited wealth was like that, and for the surviving progeny served only to blunt any trace of their ancestors' accomplishments and productivity. Most were unworthy of their birthright and, as proof, eventually their common background of privilege would fail to justify that inheritance. Though money had always served as a great cushion against failure, it only lasted so long.

As adolescents struggling to adopt an identity, neither Weezie nor Hap ever embraced any false sense of entitlement due to where their parents had chosen to live. In fact, they resented the haughtiness of some of their classmates who could not refrain from flaunting their lofty station in life. The Porter and Franklin families weren't typical. The attraction of Fox Chapel had nothing to do with climbing a social ladder or publicly displaying their relatively new-found wealth, but everything to do with enjoying the majesty of the landscape. Hobnobbing for its own sake simply wasn't who they were or how they wanted to nurture their kids. Instead, they preferred instilling the virtues of modesty, thrift, hard work, compassion, and charity in their children. Though never missing his daily scotch, Weezie recalled that her father much preferred mucking out the stalls in his barn rather than going to a cocktail party and enduring the urbane, endless chit-chat of idle gossip.

Weezie enjoyed plumbing the depths of Hap's psyche. She also found it interesting, but not troubling, that after abandoning Fox Chapel so long ago, he eventually had been drawn back to the 'hood of their upbringing. To his credit, especially given such a high public profile, she also found comfort in Hap's having done his best to remain invisible and savor his solitude.

But what had long puzzled her was how Hap could be both an introvert and extrovert. Much like her father, Weezie knew that Hap had little patience for, and couldn't abide, small talk. When at his best, Hap could feign genuine interest in the mindless ramblings of others while at the same time tuning it all out. All that changed when he took the floor. Hap's spellbound audience was captivated as he held the entire room hostage with his stories. Absent any clinical experience with what she witnessed, Weezie often wondered and at times even marveled at how Hap managed the dichotomy.

Her reflections were interrupted as Hap continued, "Look, Weeze, right now it's really rather urgent that we have a chance to talk about you know what."

"You mean what I've been dreading?"

"That and more."

"Oh God, tell me it isn't so."

"I can't now – not on an unsecured line. Just know that it's good for the country, good for the world, and good for the future of mankind."

"You forgot to say that it's good for you too, Hap."

"Yeah, hopefully there's that."

"Well that's the only part I care about. This isn't a routine mission, is it? It's the one the whole world will know about and will be talking about forever."

"Not now, Weeze, but I'll tell you when we can talk."

"You mean when you talk and I only listen."

"Something like that."

"This is insanity; I'm beginning to think you've got a death wish."

"No chance of that, at least not until the good Lord's done using me."

"For good or evil?"

"As always with this kind of work, probably a little of both."

"There's no reason for you to become a martyr just to take one bad guy out."

"But he's a very bad guy – maybe the worst ever, and I've got a lot more skin in this game than anyone else."

"And apparently enough to risk everything, including me. Why not just ease up a bit on yourself."

"How and why would I want to do that?"

"You could start by giving yourself permission not to be a savior. Go on, try it, Hap, but I bet you can't."

Hap just smiled, knowing full well that such a wager was impossible to win. Realizing he never would be able to allay Weezie's fears over the phone, Hap turned the conversation back to his initial question, hoping for a chance to sprinkle it with a little of his customary fairy dust and banter.

"So, are we on for the weekend?"

"Maybe, let me see if I can get off work."

"I'm sure I could help with that."

"Help? How?"

"By getting you off."

"That's tempting too, but would only confirm that I'd failed at resisting you."

"That's good to know, Weeze, but I don't have much more to say about that. You see, I'm a believer that there's no legitimate response to failure."

"You're so predictable."

"And doggedly persistent. Don't I get any credit for that?"

"None at all, but you do get points for maintaining your effervescence, which never seems to fizzle out. You know, my mother warned me about you."

"Really? When?"

"Oh, way back when. She said you were the kind of boy I could fall for."

"Are you sure she didn't say *should* fall for?"

"Well, that too, but that was later on when we were in college."

"Maybe you should have listened to her instead of heeding it as a warning."

"Yeah, I know that now, and maybe did back then as well. Just so you know, it was a hard fall that I've never fully recovered from."

"Is that *my* fault, Weeze? I've always thought I did my best to make it happen."

"I suppose you did, but I was…what, maybe overwhelmed by you and didn't want a partner who might smother my independence."

"So it *was* my fault."

"No, I was afraid of giving you a real chance, but after the last few years since we've been together I no longer have that fear."

"Well that's a good start. Did your mom ever say anything else?"

"Ha! Yeah, she said you had those bedroom eyes that could get a girl in trouble."

"Seems she was definitely clairvoyant."

"No, but I am, and those eyes and personality of yours still spell trouble, but of a different sort."

"I wasn't aware that I could publicly broadcast such anxiety."

"You know damn well the big trouble is the one awaiting you in Moscow."

"I can confront that."

"See, that's the problem, you really do believe in your own infallibility."

"What's the point of going to war if you don't win? Without confidence, you can't win, so what's wrong with embracing the mindset of the victor *before* the battle begins?"

"Because in this case you could just as easily become the victim. Unbridled retribution can cloud judgment."

"I've got that under control."

"Really, Hap. Since when? Though layered in artifice, your underlying rage isn't something that can be reined-in or temporarily put away."

"Now isn't that encouraging. Maybe I need a new shrink."

"There's no one out there better than I am for what you need."

"All docs tend to be overly confident in their own abilities."

"But most don't have patients as difficult as you. I have nothing more to give you than my love, but so far that apparently hasn't been enough. In some ways you're not much better than a common thief that steals something precious and priceless, only to trade it away for pennies on the dollar."

"I'm hardly squandering it, Weeze. You'll be a big incentive to return with all limbs intact and ready to move forward – hopefully unencumbered by grief and anger."

"We'll see, but then what will you do?"

"Maybe publish a comprehensive compendium of errata."

"Errata?"

"Yeah, in defense of all the damage that some suspect I've caused along the way."

"I see – a self-help book to dispel your frailties. So, would this anthology include an apology?"

"Not necessarily."

"Contrition must always precede redemption, if that's what you're looking for before the endgame."

"I really don't know how it happens, Weeze, but sometimes I keep making things worse when only trying to make things better."

"That's easy; you try too hard, so as I said earlier, ease up on yourself."

That was the way they left it – undecided as before, so it was probably best that Weezie decided not to come to Pittsburgh after all. Plus, Hap had enough to do without wondering how he could express sufficient contrition without doing too much penance.

# LOCKED AND LOADED

I~~T DIDN'T TAKE LONG FOR~~ POTUS to give the go-ahead on operation *Bad Bear Down*. Estimates of restitution to replace the physical destruction of Ukraine by Russia were being revised upward on a near-daily basis, but the human toll was incalculable. Apart from the occupation of Ukraine, wholesale genocide, and flagrant cyberterrorism, there were also direct and inhumane assaults on American citizens. Besides jailing tourists on trumped-up charges, the Czar had taken the uniquely American invention of the microwave oven and weaponized it for use against its creator.

Concentrated beams of invisible microwave energy could penetrate glass and brick, and by targeting those high doses of electromagnetic impulses on humans, it caused a variety of symptoms, including incapacitation. Since such attacks had begun in 2016 with the U.S. Embassy in Cuba, the resulting psychogenic injuries from incidents there and elsewhere were now being dubbed the Havana Syndrome. When it began happening in Washington as well, the infuriated President was even more motivated to sign off on taking Poppa Bear down.

While awaiting the President's okay, Bud's people had been working at a feverish pace to plan the operation, and it was now time to bring Hap into the fold and up to speed. Once summoned, and eager for not only the briefing, but to opine on what his intended role might be, Hap was at Langley the next day. This time he was escorted to one of the doubly secured conference rooms in the basement and joined there by the DDO along with his longtime Assistant Director, Peter Pavlovich. It was clear that it would be Pavlovich to whom Hap would now be reporting. Unaccustomed to taking direction from anyone but Bud, Hap found his new place on the totem pole dispiriting, but not enough to complain about.

Hap had worked with Pavlovich before and was respectful of his thoroughness when executing anything that fell under the unofficial black ops category. His first name was once Piotr, but he found it easier in his newly adopted home to be called Peter. Inside Langley, he was known deferentially and affectionately as Peter the Great, and when occasionally needing an informal undercover name – just Comrade. Most insiders also presumed Peter would be chosen as Bud's successor when the time came.

Pavlovich brought an extra measure of zeal to any espionage involving his one-time Russian homeland, and for good reasons. Stalin had executed his grandparents without sufficient cause, but rather on only a vague suspicion of treason. Their only son and Peter's father was mistakenly left alive as an orphan who eventually became a vocal dissident of the authoritative regimes that followed. Peter's seething, personal resentment of the current Czar was understandable. His mother and subversive father were "disappeared" forever and without a trace, but not before arranging for their only son's safe passage out of Russia. Curiously, all of this occurred about the same time that the Czar was then an ambitious lieutenant colonel among the ranks of the KGB and known for ruthless treatment of Kremlin critics.

After presenting himself at the American Embassy in West Berlin, the debriefing and ultimate defection of Piotr Pavlovich had been overseen by Bud Smith, then a passionate and persuasive recruiter for the CIA. It wasn't long before the first-ever native Russian was working for Uncle Sam in one of its most sensitive areas and later promoted to its darker side when Bud became the DDO.

As might be expected, beyond ridding his homeland of the Czar and the endemic corruption he had ushered in, Peter the Great's fervent intention was to end the suppression of human rights and restore the dignity of his people. His noble ambitions notwithstanding, Peter had something in common with Hap – a shared personal loathing of the Czar, and was not above summoning any means possible to ensure his particularly gruesome demise.

After the obligatory pleasantries, Bud began to unveil the plan.

"Hap, you'll be pleased to know that we're locked and loaded for bear without any of the usual humanitarian restrictions."

"That's a comfort, but I really wasn't planning to abide by any articles of the Geneva Convention on this trip."

"We just gotta make sure we get the right guy, which will require a DNA sample for absolute proof."

"Huh?"

"For protection, the Czar uses a lot of look-alike decoys to take his place at public events where he's expected to appear out in the open. They are very good replicas, or body doubles that serve as stunt men on occasions when he could be in jeopardy from an outside or inside assassin."

"Really? Well, I suppose that's hardly surprising, Bud."

"These clones have been re-chiseled by the world's most gifted plastic surgeons, and though not direct protégés of Dr. Josef Mengele, these reconstructive butchers borrow freely from his procedures. Their results are impressive. In fact, I'd wager their finished products would have made the Angel of Death envious."

"How did we confirm this?"

"It's been rumored for years, but we got this last year from one of the prototypes that didn't make the final cut due to permanent disfiguration in surgery, but that's not your worry. The real issue is that the Czar is always surrounded by an elaborate security detail. Fortunately, Sunny Day herself has compromised a key member."

"As well as Cherkov? I would have assumed that she'd be tasked with running the playbook and not taking on field agent assignments?"

"Like you were, and still are, Hap, she can't seem to leave the actual spook elements to her underlings. She craves the action, and is among the best at it."

"So I understand."

"She'll brief you on all aspects of the takedown once you're there, as I think it's better you remain in the dark on this for now."

"I don't like being left in the dark, and you know that."

"Like everyone else, you're on a need-to-know basis."

"Well, I *need* to know, and right now."

"Sunny will bring you up to speed in due time and I'm counting on you to follow her lead, which you've done so well in the past."

"If we were alone I'd say kiss my ass, Bud, but that's hardly something Peter should hear."

"Easy, Hap; here's something that'll make you happy. I paid a visit to your buddy Mac, and he's all in, though it's gonna cost me plenty."

"The last thing he needs is money."

"I could tell that from his chateau on the lake. What our co-pilot wants is a big favor instead, and Mac's one tough negotiator.

"Maybe you'd forgotten he has a fuckin' law degree."

"I probably did, but shoulda pegged him for one of those slippery sons of bitches. You know, Shakespeare was right about all the lawyers."

"He was right about everything, Bud, and you oughta read all his stuff. One day I'll loan you my copy of his First Folio edition."

"It wouldn't surprise me if you actually owned one, but back to your buddy Mac, do you have any advice on how to proceed with him?"

"Just be careful not to upend the scales of justice by stiffing him on any promises made or deals agreed to. Though typically a quiet and pensive kind of guy, he doesn't abide being wronged in any way. If you renege on anything, Bud, you can bet he'll come after your ass, so just keep your word and he'll hold up his end of the bargain."

"Christ, Hap, can you believe that in lieu of cash he's demanding a few rides aboard a variety of our supersonic aircraft, but with him in the driver's seat. That's gonna be a big ask when I request that from the Air Force."

"Then try the Space Force; seems they need something to do."

"It would be a lot easier to just give him an old F-15 or retired F-16 now mothballed in their boneyard base in Tucson along with a guided tour of Area 51."

"Do what it takes, Bud, but make sure whatever you end up bartering with is free. Don't forget Mac's family was in the amusement park business, so he's only accustomed to complimentary all-day gate passes and free ride tickets. Plus, if he gets to fly something like the F-22 and somehow ends up putting it nose down into the desert, the Air Force could buy a brand new bird with what Mac and I have paid in income taxes."

"Don't rub it in."

"I've never done that, Bud, because most of what I have is God-given. What I *have* done is simply always tried to do what's right. It was only recently that I learned to accept prosperity as proof of God's approval."

"Enough of your preaching; let's get back to Mac's real motivation to accept this opportunity to get himself killed."

"Seems like he gave you the answer, Bud. Remember, every pilot on earth has seen the Top Gun movies and they all want only two things outta life – to wear aviator sunglasses and see how many Gs they can pull."

"We'll see how many Machs Mac can take. Anyway, the next time you'll see him is when you're aloft and en route to bear country."

"And when will that flight be?"

"We're another couple of weeks away from takeoff, so you'd better say your goodbyes soon, but without being too specific about your hunting trip or return date. Actually, going on safari might be a good cover story and explain why you'll be unreachable while in a prolonged communication blackout."

# FAREWELL TO PROTOCOL

BIDDING A FOND ADIEU TO LINDSAY without getting caught at it would be the most difficult, so Hap decided to begin his rounds of good byes by starting with her. Knowing he had to tread lightly, he phoned her with the intention of inviting Lindsay and her daughter, Katie, for a quick visit to Fox Chapel. Hap knew she loved to come home and figured it would also give her husband a welcome respite to be alone without any childcare duties for a few days.

Unable to conceal his anxiety about the need that her visit be sooner rather than later, Lindsay was more suspicious than usual. She had always been perceptive, usually getting what information she was after in clever round-about ways by probing here and there until bringing the whole picture into sharp focus. That was okay and something Hap could deal with; it was her stubbornness that was worrisome.

"Daddy, somehow your invitation seems more like a summons."

"Well, Honey, maybe this one is a summons. Haven't I earned that right?"

"You mean privilege?"

"Of course; I suppose it could be that as well."

"Will your doctor friend be there too?"

"No, what made you ask about her?"

"Since this seems rather urgent, I thought maybe you had some important news to share."

"Nope, I just want to spend some quiet time with my daughter and granddaughter, which is probably much more than a right, and may qualify as an entitlement."

"Okay, you win. After all, I mustn't dare refuse a command performance. How about we leave tomorrow midday and arrive in time for me to cook you dinner?"

"Perfect."

"I'll text you a grocery list."

"Just make sure there's none of that organic, gluten-free or non-GMO crap on your list. You know I like the way good food used to taste when laden with yummy hormones."

"You'll live a lot longer if you'd start eating healthy food."

"So I've been told, but at my age, I need all the preservatives I can get."

"Good to know you're getting a full helping. Maybe the preservatives will make it easier to mummify you for posterity when the time comes. Another thing you might consider is becoming a vegan."

"Honey, why would I do that when in some respects I already am."

"Really?"

"Yup. All the animals I eat are vegan."

"You know, Daddy, my abiding hope is that one of these days we'll get on the same page about something."

"It'll happen a lot sooner if we were reading from any of the books in *my* library instead of yours."

"Sorry, but you're breaking up, so I'm hanging up."

"Aw, no fair; you've pulled that little trick on me before."

When younger, Lindsay would endure, but not always embrace her father's old-fashioned, if not unfashionable attempts at passing down a little unsolicited wisdom. Sometimes he could pull the wool over her eyes and get away with it, but not so much anymore. No longer naïve, she was now a strong-willed woman, and though not often admitting it aloud, he liked that about her.

They arrived the next day as promised. Beforehand, and as Lindsay knew he would, Hap had filled her entire grocery list, reluctantly including those items he neither understood nor could abide. Predictably, young Katie bounded from the car and ran to Hap's outstretched arms. Then, as had become their customary greeting, he tossed her into the air as she squealed with delight. He had never failed to catch her, and figured by the time there might be a chance of that, she would be too heavy to hoist. With hands on her hips, Lindsay looked on with mild disapproval, but tinged with happiness. She was glad to be home, if only for a day or two, and as always, wanted every minute spent with her father to be special.

Like Lindsay and Chris had before her, Katie enriched Hap's life in more ways than he could count. Watching her play and listening to her sing was magical and spellbinding. Sometimes it proved difficult because of how much she resembled her namesake and grandmother, Kate. Hap knew it must have been equally hard for Lindsay to bear the heartache along with the joy of seeing her mother's face in her own child.

After a long walk around the grounds, where Hap couldn't refrain from sharing way too much information about the constant changes he was making to the landscape, it was time for Katie's nap and some alone time for Hap and Lindsay.

"So why the sudden summons, Daddy?"

"Good grief, don't *you* get down to business in a hurry."

"I had a good teacher."

"So you did, but I'm not gonna give it up that easily, and certainly not before we engage in some playful repartee."

"Just so it doesn't become disagreeable."

"That's no fun. C'mon, Lindsay, would it kill you to work with me a little bit? Think of it as intellectual sparring, which should be child's play for you when facing an old relic like me."

"You must have been a rare archaeological marvel and real find when Mommy discovered you."

"Indeed, and I think she mistakenly took me as a gemstone in the rough that she could polish into something of value."

Knowing he would provoke her until she relented and played along, Lindsay grudgingly decided to indulge him further, but without letting on that she enjoyed the mutual ribbing as much as her father. Without conceding any ground, they did so until a silent truce indicated it was time to get serious. The last thing Hap wanted was to rattle her, but there didn't seem to be a way to avoid that, so he began with a brief, simple statement.

"I'm going to be away for a while and not likely reachable."

It was what Lindsay had dreaded for a long time and, fearing the truth, was one of those things she had managed to avoid discussing with her father. She and her brother, Christopher, had long suspected that their father was involved in something surreptitious and dangerous, but knew better than try to confront him. So, she thought, if not now, when? It was time for her Dad to come clean, though she knew he wouldn't. Nevertheless, Lindsay decided to press him for any obscure detail he might be willing to reveal.

"So, is this one of those foreign trips you used to take but shared very little about when you came home?"

"Something like that."

"Is it a dangerous destination this time?"

"Seems everywhere is these days."

"Is it the kind of place where you'd want *me* to visit?"

"Probably not, at least in the near future, but hopefully one day it will be."

"It's hard to keep pretending that all this is normal, so when are you gonna grow up, act your age, and quit this second career?"

"Soon, Honey, very soon."

"I'm not dumb enough to believe *that*."

"Believe what you must, but this time it's undeniably true; I promise."

"Good, and one more thing – remember that you don't have to keep doing something heroic to be my hero. All I need is for you to be in my life and for a long time to come."

Fighting back the tears, Hap could only smile back at his firstborn, who continued, "You know, Daddy, right now really isn't the time to go centurion on me."

"We can't *only* do the things we *want* to do in life."

"Why not?"

"Because there are some things we *must* do simply because we can."

"You don't have to be the last living dinosaur to walk the earth."

"By walking, I presume that would be upright using only the hind legs instead of all four."

"I guess so. But why?"

"Wouldn't that make me a flesh-eating Tyrannosaurus Rex, or king of all creatures great and small?"

"Okay, once again I bow to your logic."

"Not so fast, Honey Bun. This isn't the time for you to *finally* show some decorous behavior; you can't give up by quitting on me so soon."

"Only if you quit making it so hard for all of us to be proud of you."

"I'll do what I can, but it's me who's brimming with pride."

"About what?"

"I got to be your dad. Now give me a hug and we'll talk about this no more."

Sometimes that was the way they left things – understood but unspoken. His message got through; at least that was Hap's take on it. One day he would try to get her to confirm that, but now wasn't the time.

# CLOSURE UP CLOSE

WORRIED THAT THE SCHISM between them was widening to the point where neither of them might take any remedial steps to repair it, Louise phoned Hap, but not until after downing a glass of Chardonnay.

"Benjamin Harrison Franklin, I think it's my turn to issue you a formal invitation."

"To what, where, and when, my dear Dr. Porter?"

"Cocktails, right now, but I suspect with you far away in Fox Chapel, that's impossible."

"Ha, just so happens I'm in Washington, so I could be there in less than an hour if you can hold off on having that second glass of wine."

"How'd you know that?"

"I'm good at recognizing the power of social lubricants. I can hear it in your voice and almost smell it on your breath."

"What you're really good at, Hap, is observation, even when you're guessing. Anyway, I'll just kick off my shoes and await your arrival."

"But please – only your shoes and nothing else. I'll take care of the rest."

"À bientôt, mon ami."

With Weezie, Hap knew it took only one glass of white wine to warm her up into a playful mood. And when she started including some French in her conversation, the signals were unmistakable. But no matter how tempting, it would be important in the long run for him not to take advantage of her hospitality in any way. That didn't stop him from taking a quick shower, changing into a better set of clothes, and splashing on some cologne. As always, it was Old Spice, which he knew drove her wild but didn't know why – maybe only because it was old. Beyond being a familiar fragrance, its other purpose was to counter what his face now looked like.

Hap had stopped shaving two weeks earlier to begin growing the full beard that would become part of his cover. To his surprise, the whiskers were coming in very fast, but in a light gray, and some places even snowy white. This minor change to what had become a daily routine since a teenager proved not only annoyingly itchy, but served to age him beyond his years. To be sure, the grizzled face made him look more like a hobo than the dashing flight commander he was about to impersonate. He was told to let it grow out everywhere and not dare touch it. Langley's make-up team would trim and tint it to their liking, but in the meantime, he didn't like it one bit. When Weezie answered the door, it was clear from the shock on her own face that she didn't either.

"Well now, I wasn't expecting a total stranger, Hap. What's this, your new Hollywood look?"

"Well, yes and no, but so far the new persona hasn't yet worked on any women. When it was only stubble, I was expecting lots of booty calls, but got nary a one, so I was hoping you'd fall for it and give me a big sloppy kiss."

"That's something I can do, but anything beyond a little smooch will depend on your behavior."

"Oh don't worry, I know better than to try to hit on you in your condition, Dr. Porter – not to mention how scandalous that'd be for you if your neighbors are watching."

They embraced and Weezie delivered on her promise. Though shorter than he was used to, the kiss felt good, and they both knew it. It had been a long time since they had tasted each other, and it showed in their glowing faces and probably quickened heart rates as well.

It was clear from Hap's budding disguise that he was in the final stages of preparation for the mission and likely imminent departure. Louise knew there would be no stopping him, even with the threat of an ultimatum. Resigned to the fact that Hap would be leaving and may not return, this time she refrained from asking all the questions she desperately wanted him to answer. Instead, the evening was more like all the good times they had spent together over the last few years.

They shared news of their children, her crazy patients, and what was blooming in his garden – all peppered with the spirited and frisky jousting they so enjoyed when alone. Despite her apprehensions about the future, if this were to be their last time together, she wanted it to be a joyful send-off that each would treasure forever. Louise did have a few questions that she hoped wouldn't be controversial, but instead might get Hap to talk about the fears she knew he harbored. Despite knowing full well that going there would be a sticky wicket, she did so anyway.

"So, Hap, how will you ever fit in over there?"

"In my experience, sometimes the best way to blend in is to stick out, so I'll just be myself."

"Oh, you mean clever and cavalier or just plain bombastic?"

"Maybe a slightly watered-down version of both."

"And you think that'll improve your chance of survival?"

"It's always worked in the past."

"But not always without some remnants of collateral harm."

"What harm?"

"The vestiges of permanent injury to yourself and those who love you."

"I'll be careful, and after all, my role is removing only part of the world's wickedness."

"But a big part."

"It has to be done now that the Administration finally understands that it can't reason with evil. Our job at Langley is to examine everything that's wrong in the world and then coach the President along by helping him decide which ones to act upon. Basically, we act as an ombudsman when he needs encouragement to either pull the plug or pull the trigger."

"Then you're a good man after all?"

"Not always; the problem is that sometimes good men have to do bad things."

"But Hap, the difference is that good men *have* to, whereas bad men *choose* to, so having to do evil doesn't diminish your goodness."

"But I'll eventually pay for it just the same."

"Why?

"Though Bud keeps reminding me that it's what we do but not who we are, some of those bad things weren't okay with me, so I suspect none of them would pass muster with the Almighty."

"No one's gonna sprinkle a little holy water on your sins and make them go away, but isn't God always about grace and forgiveness?"

"You're suggesting I can go to my grave with the assurance of a big pardon?"

"Not suggesting, promising. Searching for your soul will be penitence enough, Hap. For now, I just want you to be the very best you can be."

"Maybe my best isn't good enough for you. Anyway, you sound like my mother when delivering her daily *good, better, best – never let it rest* line."

"Then she must have loved you as much as I do."

Without responding, but with a pensive look, Hap threw down the last of the vodka in one gulp. His mercurial reaction made it clear to Louise that she would be unable to maneuver the conversation to places he refused to go. She had tried her best to be assertive, but had sense enough to know when to quit.

After a third glass of wine, and in a casual, matter-of-fact way, she asked Hap if he would carry her upstairs and put her to bed. After gazing intently at each other for a few moments, Hap scooped her up, and with her hands wrapped around his neck, he ascended the staircase to her boudoir. When she disappeared into the bathroom, he didn't follow, but awaited her return. The sight was well worth the wait, as she emerged in a plain white nightgown trimmed in lace. It was the one she had worn that first time in Bar Harbor. Weezie made her way slowly to the bed and crawled under the covers.

"You do recognize the flimsy nightie, right?"

"How could I ever forget that. After three days of freezing my ass off you finally offered me the warmth, comfort, and hospitality of your bed."

"That was because I needed enough time to decide if I still liked you after 30 years. But now convinced that I do, you're in luck, as history may repeat itself tonight…however, only if you're so inclined."

"I've always been inclined to recline with you, Weeze."

"Then come get me."

Just sitting at the bottom of her bed proved exciting beyond belief, knowing that his recent musings were about to become a reality. The sexual tension between them had been brewing long enough and it was now time for the momentous resumption of their complete union.

Hap stood to disrobe, slowly unbuttoned his shirt, and tossed it to the floor. After undoing his pants, he allowed them to fall, revealing the obvious surge from beneath his silken boxers. Weezie could feel the sudden warmth of overwhelming desire emanating from her entire body, almost as if a fever had taken hold. By now his growing manhood had found its way through the opening in his shorts, and as always, her eyes visibly widened at the sight.

"Don't be alarmed, Weeze. After all, it's your exuberance that brings it out from hiding."

"Is that a self-guided missile?"

"No, but it is heat-seeking. However, it may require some manual guidance to make sure it hits the right target."

"None of its possible destinations would be wrong ones and all would be immeasurably pleasurable, but if you're offering me a choice, I do have a favorite place."

"You'll have plenty of time to steer it where it's supposed to go, but not right now, as I want to prepare the way first."

"Oh, Hap, how long are you gonna make me wait?"

"Until it's time, and just to satisfy my curiosity, have you always been so easily excitable?"

"Only since meeting you in the seventh grade when I somehow knew you were destined to be unappeasingly horny forever."

"Gosh, that's not how I remember it at all, but perhaps my recall has something to do with what Mark Twain once said."

"And what was that?"

"The older I get, the more clearly I remember things that never happened."

Patiently and methodically, Hap untucked the comforter and top sheet from the foot of the bed while rolling them forward, but only until reaching her calves. His work was about to begin, and she knew he would be the one controlling the pace of her growing frenzy. Weezie was not only happy, but relieved that someone else was taking charge.

Hap slipped out of his boxers, and then tossed them to her with the instruction to cover her eyes. Weezie did as she was told, and once blindfolded, he began massaging her feet and ankles while sucking each toe. Her breathing now heavy, Hap continued the trajectory of his nuzzling up her legs while rolling the bedding forward as he moved closer to what they both knew he was after.

"Hap, your beard feels so scratchy down there."

"Don't fret, the next time we meet it'll probably just tickle instead."

"Oh good, something else to look forward to, as I've never before laughed out loud during sex."

"Thanks for the warning. I'll make a note not to take it the wrong way when you do."

Weezie instinctively drew her knees up into position, allowing Hap to slowly spread them wide with both hands to reveal the ultimate prize. He stared longingly and lovingly at the sight of her femininity before bringing his head down for a closer examination. Gently separating the lips with his thumbs, he opened her like a careful gardener might the petals of a fragrant flower to experience its majesty.

His tongue was the first to penetrate and explore the hidden treasure within. After swirling it round and round as her panting grew frantic, it was soon drawn to the sweet spot and governor of her passion. Focusing only on that trigger eventually drew the continuous flow of sweetness that would serve to ease the way for what was coming next.

What had so far been Weezie's repetitive undulations had now grown to uncontrollable heaving, but Hap was not about to be rushed. He knew full well that extending the anticipation would further fuel the fire of desire that had been burning within them for too long. Fully aware of what was ahead, he would make her wait a bit longer, as his work was far from over. When it was, she became uncontrollable, and turned Hap over on his back so she could assume her favored spot atop him. Once fully seated, she hammered him home to exhaustion until both of their bodies were weary and limp. For Hap it seemed like their union had been overcharged with an intensity like never before.

For some, sex was too often an ephemeral experience because just like that, it was over. But for Hap and Weezie, the extended afterglow of euphoria which followed was almost as pleasurable. After relishing the emotional, but unspoken, post-coital sentiments that always accompanied her times with Hap, Louise was the first to interrupt the stillness.

"I have a confession."

"Uh oh, don't tell me I failed to make the grade this time."

"Hardly, but I *am* surprised that we do this so well at our ages."

"Maybe it's just muscle memory."

"I don't think so, especially given your continued innovation in such matters. More likely it's yet another manifestation of your performative nature."

"I do what I can to change it up from time to time, but couldn't do so without your inspiration."

"All I do is follow your lead and respond reciprocally. You know, Hap, there will come a day when I'll lose those capacities of inducement."

"Hopefully not in my lifetime. I'd be content to manifest myself in any one of your favorite positions indefinitely."

"I may have to rely on your patience and sagacity when the time comes. But for now, I'll take the sailor with only one night's shore leave."

"No problem. But before we attempt an encore, is there anything else you want to get off your chest while closeted in my cozy confessional? Maybe that you're tired of putting up with me."

"No, nothing like that, but something more alarming – lately I've been having nightmares."

"I didn't know shrinks got them; I thought they only explained them."

"Be serious for once. My premonitions are all about you not coming back."

"You don't need to worry about that. There's too much waiting for me here – especially you."

"When you come back, will you come straight to me?"

"Not only to you; I'll come straight for you."

"You'd better."

# DRESS REHEARSAL

Hap spent the next week at Fort Meade prepping for anything that might go sideways and spoil the mission. It was the usual drill before any overseas departure by a clandestine asset. His stay included a comprehensive update on the latest technology he might encounter, which was what usually ensnared spies once an enemy feared they were up to no good. Due to Hap's disdain for all things techie, Bud was taking no chances, and to drive the point home, had insisted Hap take a crash course in the newest countersurveillance techniques.

Because of its sheer size and available acreage to grow even larger, many of the CIA's operations had been relocated from Langley to Fort Meade. Much like Camp Peary had long been commonly referred to as *The Farm*, Fort Meade was called *The Fort* by insiders. It was there that the old Office of Technical Resources, or OTS as Hap couldn't refrain from still calling it, was now housed.

As with the burgeoning federal budget, even the OTS's official name had been expanded and was now The Directorate of Science and Technology. As if that wasn't enough, some of what OTS used to do had been offloaded into a new and fifth CIA division entitled The Directorate of Digital Innovation. Between the two, they worked on anything that was conceivable and, to Hap, their labors seemed to echo Pablo Picasso's claim that "everything you can imagine is real."

Though never admitting it to Bud, Hap always enjoyed his visits to the Fort. As Albert Einstein had maintained, "creativity was intelligence having fun", and simply being a first-hand witness to the myriad activities at the Fort's laboratories was fun for the onlooker as well. The many digital enhancements to traditional tradecraft tools Hap had used over the years were astonishing. So far, he had managed to avoid most of their sophisticated gizmos, relying instead on his wits and cunning when under pressure. But because now there was little that could be hidden or disguised, the CIA's focus at the Fort was more on developing countersurveillance measures. The transition from creating innovative instruments of interrogation to protecting an agent's vulnerability was a complete one, as everything today was about building defensive precautions against an enemy presumed to have the same toys.

With the advent of wireless and Bluetooth technology, mobile collection platforms enabled spying to be done autonomously. Tiny drones, often disguised as bumble bees, could get much closer to a target than a remote camera. The bee's oversized eyes were actually high resolution 3D cameras, and it's legs hypersensitive laser microphones that, when affixed to the outside of a glass window, could hear everything going on behind it. Under the assumption that their adversaries had the same equipment, the OTS had worked equally hard to develop ways to defeat the drones.

Some of what had been invented at the Fort and elsewhere over the years by the CIA and Defense Department, but often funded through other channels of government largesse, was purposeful – like GPS and duct tape. Other things, such as microwave ovens and Super Glue, were discovered by accident.

Initially created to enable satellite guidance systems for precise targeting of military weaponry, now anyone with a smartphone had GPS. Hap was one of only a few on the planet who still relied on maps and, when the free ones that were once available in racks at filling stations were discontinued, he bought leather-bound Rand McNally atlases for all of his cars. A map was permanent, could not be corrupted, and he liked looking at the bigger picture when mapping out a journey.

Hap smiled to himself while recalling how he had tried to share his love of maps when planning how best to reach the destination of a family vacation. Unfortunately, his chosen itineraries only served to antagonize Kate and the kids, as Hap usually took the less traveled and more scenic routes rather than the fastest and most direct ones suggested by their cellphones.

Some of the discoveries made by the mad scientists had eventually advanced in deadly ways. After revolutionizing cooking for a generation, microwave technology had taken a sinister turn when the Russians found a way to corrupt it by focusing concentrated lethal beams to sicken human beings. They had done so successfully in assaults on U.S. embassies, where powerful doses could penetrate walls to inflict temporary incapacitation, if not permanent harm to the brain.

After the mandatory thorough briefings were completed, Hap had an extra day to reflect on the risks and prepare himself mentally for what was ahead. The entire mission would take ten days if all went as planned, but the slightest change or hiccup in any of the variables could change that. If so, he could be marooned in a very dangerous place until another opportunity arose for the take down. Never before had he been off the grid without a secure way of communicating for so long a period. Besides the isolation and vulnerability, snuffing out Poppa Bear would be harder than an unsuspecting target because the suspicious Czar was always on high alert.

Unlike prior assignments, Hap knew this one would be his last, and because of the long odds, he wanted it to go exceptionally well because his unblemished reputation was at stake. It had been that way with other things Hap once enjoyed, or at least thought he had. Playing golf was among the first casualties. It wasn't that he couldn't – he just didn't want to anymore. With golf, he had known when it was time to quit. This time felt different, and maybe because time was something he may be running out of. No matter what the apprehensions, Hap only hoped to return in time for curtain call on closing night to take the final bow in a play that had enjoyed a record run.

At last, it was time for final reflections, and Hap's were considered in the same order as he had catalogued them on his things-to-do list a few weeks earlier. He had made peace with Christopher and Lindsay, or at least tried to in his own way, which was the only way he knew how. His estate plans were up to date, and a handful of intimate unmailed letters had been written, but were not to be posted by his housekeeper unless he failed to return.

Always the opportunistic investor, Hap's thoughts included the allure of making a different kind of killing. In one respect, it would be the ultimate triumph over death, but in this case, the Czar's. The temptation to profit from what he was about to do was appealing, but Hap knew it was not the right thing to do. If, or rather when, the bear went down, initial fears of instability would tank world financial markets, but when the turbulence subsided, things would calm down. Once the pundits understood that a new order was firmly established in place of the old, a resumption of normalcy would occur and order would prevail. Such widespread buoyancy would propel the markets to new all-time highs, and those who bet on the rebound rewarded accordingly. How perverse that the removal of a repressive autocratic dictator would trigger explosive growth of capitalism by ushering in a prolonged bull market induced only by optimism instead of fundamentals.

*Buy the rumor and sell the fact* – that had always been how savvy traders got rich. Financial markets were driven by multiple factors, not the least of which was rapacious greed that chased turmoil. Sure, it would be an easy opportunity to make some big dough in a hurry, but Hap considered it too much like insider trading. This time it wasn't another of his hunches – it was a certainty, but cashing in big time to make a small fortune didn't seem fair. Besides, finally getting the monkey off his back would be more than enough payoff.

Tomorrow he would be flown directly from Andrews to the Royal Air Force base outside London where Cherkov's jetliner was being upgraded for its role. There he would be sequestered until it was wheels up for the oligarch's estate in the heavily forested outskirts of Moscow.

# UP, UP AND AWAY

WHEN LIVERIED IN THE NAVY BLUE UNIFORM adorned with gold braid and now sporting a full beard, Hap looked the part of a fiercely handsome commander and could have passed for any experienced, no-nonsense Aeroflot pilot. The artistry of the makeup team had been outstanding, having successfully transformed him into a character even he didn't immediately recognize when seeing a complete stranger's reflection in the mirror.

It was now rug-cutting time. Bud accompanied him from the hanger to the tarmac, all the while beseeching Hap to follow the plan, behave himself, and try to return in one piece. Hap understood that this was Bud's normal and overly pedagogical way of wishing him good luck. Nonetheless, he bristled at Bud's attempt to be fatherly in such circumstances. As was always the case, Hap struggled with taking advice despite knowing that this time it was sound and sincere.

When they parted, the newly minted and imposing imposter of a commander couldn't resist saluting the DDO as a parting gesture of deference, friendship, and playful comedy. After turning on his heels with mocking military precision, Hap climbed the steep rollaway gangway, and once inside the plane, instinctively looked left into the cockpit. As he would be, there was Mac with the thick Boeing manual on his lap busily double checking the long list of pre-flight procedures and testing the aircraft's readiness for the journey. Hap hadn't seen his old chum since before the pandemic, so even a reunion under such circumstances was a welcome one. Mac looked younger than his years, which may have reflected his excitement over the drama that awaited when crossing Russian airspace in a bird he never should have agreed to fly.

Sharing a common childhood often forged a special, if not sacred, bond of kindred friendship. It had been like that for Mac and Hap, and to an extent with Hap and Weezie as well. Having been reared under the same discipline which accompanied their shared values, these relationships had been built upon a durable bedrock foundation that was further buttressed over time. The post-war period had a profound and indelible influence on decisions that were once ahead, but now mostly behind, them. For the most part, baby boomers understood the difference between right and wrong, good and bad, and love and hate. They had respect for authority, law, and order accompanied by a strong belief in, and an abiding reverence for, their Creator. Their formative years happened in a long forgotten, if not obsolete, past. It was a time before parents became overly permissive and allowed their kids to stray from the straight and narrow course their elders had followed.

For Hap's generation, the benefit of that strict parental cultivation mostly resulted in lives well lived, though at the time they may not have expressed appropriate appreciation for that experience. But given the troubling false dialogues absorbed by today's youth, where much of their education was delivered by social media platforms, it was not surprising that they were having difficulty differentiating between truth and falsehood.

Along the way both Hap and Mac had made the tough choices in life based on that same historical framework of reference. But no matter how distinguished, when using the yardstick of that upbringing to measure his own life, Hap knew some of his choices had not been good ones, and he was far from done wrestling with God over them.

Trading stories from the past was commonplace and great fodder for a good laugh. For some of the tales, telling the truth alone was sufficiently outrageous when repeating the story. Others required some editorial exaggeration, which was never a problem for accomplished storytellers like Mac and Hap. Recollections always included a judicious mix of fact, fiction and fantasy. Eventually the distinctions became inseparable, so their reminiscences morphed into the lore they now believed was all but true.

This time Hap knew the adventure ahead of them would need no additional hype, if and when either of them ever chose to share it. Eager to get the first word in, Hap was the first to speak when greeting his old friend.

"Hey flyboy, are you still taking testosterone supplements?"

"No, but with so much to spare, my doc said I could be a donor for guys like you, Hap."

"Good, as I usually run a quart low. I hope you brought your acoustic guitar along for some in-flight entertainment."

"Sorry, I was told to pack sparingly, so just a harmonica."

"But a guitar is light, and when accompanied by harmonica, you could have serenaded us with the Appalachian version of *Love Me Do*."

"Yeah, well maybe next time, Hap, since I knew it wouldn't fit in the overhead bin and wasn't about to check any luggage on *this* airline."

"I do the same, it's called a Go Bag in spook parlance."

Mac stood, emerged from the cabin and they shook hands, which was what men used to do before hugging became acceptable. Excepting the extra stripes on Mac's shoulders that designated his stature as a captain, their identical designer uniforms were of better quality and far more snazzy than those worn by commercial pilots. This was not surprising, as the tailors at MI6 rivaled those who fashioned bespoke suits on Savile Row.

Emblazoned with the Russian flag and the moniker of the Cherkov Group's corporate logo on the lapels, no expense was spared when costuming the American actors.

"Hap, in case you don't know it, you look a little rough today, especially with that scruffy beard and ill-fitting rug on your head. I'm guessing Bud told ya his team could make you look a whole lot better and you foolishly believed him. You *really* shouldn't let your vanity take over when getting dressed, so promise me next time you won't."

"Trust me, Mac, even on your best day you'd need more than a complete overhaul to look as good as I do on a bad day."

"Not looking like you do now. Maybe it's because you're not getting enough beauty sleep."

"I get plenty of bed rest, Mac."

"But let me guess – not enough sleep."

"Even when sleep-deprived I'm better looking than you – always was and always will be."

"Not according to the girls back in high school."

"No way, Mac, I'm pretty sure I would've won the popular vote in a landslide."

"Only if the boys voted."

Both of them laughed at Mac's sharp-witted rejoinder, but Hap had to admit, if only to himself, that Mac's youthful boyish grin and dry humor may have given him a slight edge in those days. Their competitiveness had reached its zenith and ended in a draw during senior year in high school. They both were dating varsity cheerleaders who were also the brightest and best looking of the bunch, so pretty much the crème de la crème. While it lasted it was like livin' the dream.

As if on parade, showcasing these exceptional trophies on their arms for public display should have been enough of a reward. After all, going steady implied a lot of things, but mostly a visible symbol that Hap and Mac were getting something special that the others weren't. Unfortunately, when it came to putting out, that wasn't the case at all.

Though no doubt equally hot and bothered at that age after the estrogen had kicked in, neither of the gals was willing to throw aside her pompoms, hike up her skirt and give it away too soon. Maintaining the myth of promiscuity was all about feeding the curiosity, but mostly envy, of their male classmates. This certainly wasn't the kind of secret that *ever* needed to be disclosed and thereby spoil the boys' reputations. And so far, despite the passage of so many years, neither Hap nor Mac had given it up to the other or anyone else.

"Also, and in case you've forgotten, Mac, *mine* was the head cheerleader."

"I never knew what that meant, but probably only a titular title. Speaking of titles, didn't they tell you that my new name for this voyage is Nikolai? For you, Cap'n will do, but a full salute when addressing me would be even better."

"If you were a bird colonel I'd be more than willing to give you the bird, but that's the extent of my formal training in military etiquette. So, you're now Nikolai, huh? I'm guessing Langley named you after that cheap-ass vodka and it's likely the only Russian word you know."

"Actually, Hap, I don't drink anymore."

"But I bet you don't drink any less."

"Don't have to, as these days I get the same woozy effect from just standing up too fast."

"You know, Mac, I'm surprised you're not on a walker by now. By the way, I warned Bud that you might be a quick study in some things, but mastering *any* foreign language wasn't in your wheelhouse."

"Is that the gratitude I get for letting you talk me into this? Just so ya know, besides my new temporary name, I happen to know lots of Russkie words."

"Like what?"

"Well, let's see…besides Beef Stroganoff, there's Glasnost, Perestroika, Kalashnikov, Sputnik, and of course Russian Roulette."

"Mighty impressive, Nikolai, and my apologies; seems you're all set for infiltration and obviously over-prepared for any possible interrogation."

"Enough of this, Hap, I've got my own marching orders, so get your bony ass into bed; there's an unbelievable rack all the way in the back. We'll try to avoid any turbulence so you're not aroused until touchdown. This flying hotel is a real testimony to unnecessary splendor, even before being equipped with more practical accessories like stealth, radar-jamming, and some other classified defense systems options."

"Somehow I knew those things would turn you on."

"Oh, and speaking of getting turned on, there's another outstanding feature to this ride. Her name's Natalya, and you'll get a stiff Molotov cocktail after meeting her."

"I'm up for both, and glad to see you know yet another Russian word. Now if anything goes haywire, Nikolai, try to remember to throw the right switch at the right time. These won't be the friendly skies you're used to."

"This beast almost flies itself, but I'd better get back to rereading the flight manual in case we encounter any problems. Plus, I gotta keep my eye on Cherkov's pilot – one wrong move and he's a goner."

"One more thing, Nikolai. While I'm on assignment you should check every square inch of this plane for anything that shouldn't be aboard during our return flight."

"What am I looking for?"

"Anything that might bring it down. In case you don't know, when assets become liabilities, the CIA isn't above burning them, and with the fallout from a mission of this magnitude, they wouldn't hesitate to extinguish any and all evidence of culpability."

"Really? I didn't sign up for engaging any friendly fire from the good guys."

"It's just a remote possibility in case anything goes wrong on my end."

"Well you'd better make damn sure it doesn't."

Hap meandered his way back through the aircraft, which was indeed a spectacle of opulence on display. Cherkov had spared no expense to make the interior lavish, if not gaudy. It reminded Hap of the same garish decor of the former U.S. President, who was always itching to show off the gilded furniture and tasteless glitter adorning his New York penthouse to journalists and photographers. The showy, but worthless appointments throughout the plane were just so much trumpery, which was a word used for centuries before the former president fully embraced its meaning.

Having been aboard Air Force One a few times, Hap couldn't help but compare its practicality and underwhelming comfort to the showy ostentation of the oligarch's clown car with wings. There was a strict pecking order for boarding, seating, and deplaning on the presidential aircraft. Staff members, occasional congressional guests and the omnipresent gaggle of reporters had to be aboard and back in steerage long ahead of the president's arrival. To satisfy the cameras that yearned to capture such meaningless pageantry, the commander in chief was always the last to board and first to depart. The photo ops also served to remind all whose plane it was.

This time there was no parade of onlookers. Hap was the only passenger, and though disguised to appear as the required, but unnecessary, third pilot, the owner's cabin was all his to experience. Unlike the president's queen bed in Air Force One, Cherkov's was a canopied king-size with 600-thread count Egyptian cotton sheets. The bedding, pillows and comforter were all embroidered with the same logo and insignia as Hap's counterfeit pilot's jacket.

Soon after changing into comfortable loungewear, a soft knock was heard at the door and, before he could answer, a tall, raven-haired raving beauty let herself in. Though clad in what never would have passed for a commercial flight attendant's outfit, she would have as easily been as fetching if wearing a peasant's babushka and barn coat. Beyond her legs, most of which were visible due to the short leather skirt, the tight silk bodice also clung to what it was never intended to hide from speculation. She paused long enough for Hap to take it all in before introducing herself and explaining her role, but he preempted her.

"Wait; let me guess, you must be Natalya."

"And you are obviously well informed, Commander. I will be at your service for anything you might desire during and perhaps after the flight. But first, beyond your beverages of choice from the bar, I'll be serving you filet and lobster."

"We call that surf and turf back home."

"As do we, Commander."

Clearly, Hap's feeble attempt at humor wasn't working, but apparently that wasn't going to be necessary with Natalya, who asked only if he'd like to be served now or later, reminding him that the flight would be less than four hours long. Following a perfect vodka martini, the meal was accompanied by both red and white wines along with an assortment of sides that were equally outstanding. Moments after he had finished eating she returned to clear the sterling silver place settings and antique English bone china dinnerware.

"Will there be anything else, Commander? Perhaps some dessert?"

"Not this time; I'll just nap until we land."

Though well aware that anything beyond serving his dinner was just part of her job, Hap could see the disappointment in her face as she lingered a bit to see if he might change his mind. He wouldn't be, but nonetheless had enjoyed her straightforward and predatory approach.

"I will be just outside your door should you need anything. And remember that nothing you wish for would be an inconvenience for me, but rather a privilege."

Following the encounter with Natalya, Hap was understandably unable to sleep, which gave him an opportunity to meditate further on why the success of *Bad Bear Down* was so imperative. Besides, it wasn't that unusual for him to require last-minute justification before a kill, if only to placate any remaining traces of self-doubt. Labeling the operation anything other than state-sponsored terrorism would be a lie and, despite supportive global sentiment, that wasn't something he or America ever wanted to be accused of. Though the rationale was sound, there would never be complete vindication for what Hap was about to do. Nevertheless, beyond taking the life of the one who took Kate's, he considered the constellation of other factors that might lessen the burden of committing yet another cardinal sin in service to his country.

Eliminating the world's most offensive despot and dismantling his totalitarian regime was paramount. And because the Czar would never be tried or face the gallows for his heinous crimes of slaughtering innocent civilians in Ukraine, Russia and elsewhere, there was only one remaining remedy – the single sanction of permanent censure, which was CIA jargon for assassination.

The Czar's playbook wasn't too far flung from the pathological former U.S. president's – pervasive criminality and prolonged ideological warfare by spreading disinformation. But unlike the former president's ongoing spew of polarizing rhetoric and demagoguery since leaving the White House, the Czar's authoritarian populism couldn't continue from the grave.

Unfortunately for America, its deposed leader lived like an uncrowned king and continued to cast an enormous, unforgiveable shadow on democracy while raising a gargantuan personal war chest by mining the pocketbooks of those least able to afford it. He too would not live forever, but his antithetical legacy might survive among enough dangerous followers to wreak additional homegrown havoc. Such extremist perspectives were enough to stoke growing apprehension about the future while sowing additional seeds of insurrection.

Hap must have been dozing, as suddenly he was awakened from slumber by Mac's familiar voice – spoken in English but with a bad fake Russian accent.

"Commander Franklin, all is well from the flight deck, and though I can only imagine what's going on back there, we've cleared airspace and are being vectored in for final approach. I thought you might like to join us up front for landing, as it'll be a lot more exciting than when I used to put these big birds down at Sheremetyevo."

Hap knew communication with the tower would have been in English, as it was the global standard used by all air traffic controllers when speaking with pilots worldwide. It was presumed that the Russian flying left seat would conduct the conversations, with his copilot Mac serving only as a backup if the Russkie were incapacitated for any reason. Given Mac's laughable forgery of a Russian accent, Hap figured that hadn't been necessary.

When emerging from the bedroom suite, and as expected, Hap found Natalya languishing in a fully reclining seat nearby. Having kicked off her high heels during the flight, she jumped to her bare feet and longingly stared somewhat longer than necessary before reminding Hap that she would be on call during his visit to the Cherkov estate. Though he knew her services would not be called upon, Hap decided to reward her attempts at seduction by giving her a peck on the forehead. When doing so, she rose up on her stockinged tiptoes so that her mouth could meet his instead, but Hap refused that proposition as well.

Hap reached the flight deck in time to take in the panorama of Moscow. From the sky it looked no different than any other city, but it gave him shivers anyway. Soon after their final descent a few minutes later, Cherkov's sprawling dacha came into view, together with runway lights ablaze to assure a soft touch down. After taxying to an enormous hanger, the plane was towed inside where its owner anxiously awaited his new house guests.

To keep Cherkov waiting and in suspense, Hap insisted on being the last to deplane. Reluctantly, he shook the outstretched bionic right hand and said nothing, but the suspicion on his face said everything.

"Come now, Commander, in this new spirit of détente we are at last collaborators, so let's forget the past and look toward a bright future where both of us can prosper and enjoy the time we have left."

"Over the years I've learned to trust no one, and that includes you, Ivan."

"Please, call me Dmitri, though I know the CIA once dubbed me Ivan the Terrible."

"If the shoe fits, Ivan."

"Enough of this, Franklin. I'd love to give you a tour, but you must leave now for the rendezvous point. Until you return, your Captain Nikolai will be treated like royalty."

"Good, because he's used to that at home."

A custom stretch Mercedes with tinted bulletproof windows pulled alongside the Dreamliner and one of the three beefy body guards stowed Hap's luggage in its trunk. Another held the door as Hap slid in while never taking his steely eyes off Cherkov, but all the while knowing that any score he might want to settle with Ivan wouldn't happen this time.

Painstaking coordination of the smallest details was imperative when executing any field operation, but especially one of such proportion. The flight from London had been timed to arrive in the wee hours of the morning so that Hap could immediately be transferred to a dingy garage in a blighted, if not squalid, section of Moscow that housed a cleaning company. Using Cherkov's private limousine to deliver Hap there would ensure that the marked vehicle would not be stopped for any reason. Arriving in the dead of night also would provide the blanketed cover of darkness. After circling the block to make sure the streets were empty, a signal was sent and the garage door opened as Hap was rushed inside while Ivan's goons sped away in the Mercedes.

The garage was inconspicuous from the outside but, in stark contrast to what could be found behind other doors in such a grimy and gritty neighborhood, its interior was altogether different. Stocked with props of all kinds and several vehicles, Hap guessed the spotless, well-appointed workshop functioned as a secret staging area for a variety of CIA maneuvers. Seated next to the kind of adjustable chairs found in a hair salon was a makeover artist ready to further transform Hap's disguise – this time by applying a fresh façade that would include a new latex face. In a few hours dawn would arrive and, after a change of clothes, he would be dressed in the same drab uniform as the others who cleaned the CIA station chief's home away from home.

# HIDE AND SEEK

As with all spies, but especially a station chief, Sunny had deep diplomatic cover as a nondescript, lowlife State Department employee at the U.S. Embassy in Moscow. The only difference was that her status warranted additional round-the-clock surveillance by clandestine agents under her command. There were few secrets in the intelligence game, and the Americans were not among the best at keeping them. It was no surprise that the Russians knew her real purpose in Moscow, and they too kept many eyes trained on Sunny and her security detail. Beyond being tracked daily by spooks from the Russian Federal Security Service, there were multiple surveillance cameras surrounding her apartment that sent a continuous feed to Lubyanka Square.

However, once inside, Sunny could relax and speak freely without fear of unwelcome eavesdropping by her Russian counterparts. The buildout of certain renovations to her apartment had been performed by a trusted American contractor and overseen by the CIA. Its construction included an elaborate metal spiderweb within the walls and sophisticated jamming equipment that prevented any outside attempts to listen in.

Though having Hap hide out at Sunny's apartment was Bud's idea, it was also the safest place for a temporary safe house to lodge someone who should never have been in Moscow in the first place. Getting Hap inside and away from the prying street cameras was a challenge all by itself. As with other high-ranking officials of the embassy, Sunny was provided weekly complimentary maid service that was performed by discreet embassy employees.

It was assumed the Russkies knew this too, which accounted for their utmost vigilance when the cleaning crew came and went on their usual day, which for Sunny was always on Fridays.

The cleaning crew's size varied from week to week – sometimes two and occasionally three. Fortunately, the crew always parked in Sunny's garage and thereby could only be seen and sometimes photographed by the hawk-eyed Russian observers through the vehicle's windows when arriving and departing. On this day three cleaners arrived, but only two departed – that is, if not counting their motionless third companion in the back seat – an inflatable decoy resembling the one who was staying behind.

Once safely inside, Hap had nothing to do but unpack and relax until Sunny arrived home from the embassy. She would do so at her usual time to avoid any unnecessary curiosity from the FSB's rotating surveillance teams that shadowed her comings and goings for anything out of the ordinary. The guest room where his luggage had been taken by one of the cleaners was spacious, well-appointed, and comfortable. Both the blinds and fashionable balloon shade window draperies had already been closed to help keep his residency a secret from any outside onlookers.

Hap was anxious to remove all elements of the disguise he had worn since crossing the border. The latex mask and makeup proved hotter than he was led to believe, and his native skin underneath was beginning to itch. Weary of the fake contact lenses that made his eyes water, he took them out as well. The adhesive that kept the hairpiece in place was painful to remove and required alcohol to do so. When unable to find any, he substituted with some 176-proof Bulgarian vodka from the bar. It was a far better solution than yanking the glue off and risking the loss of what little hair he had left on top.

How odd that Hap had long hair until he was married, and then…well, he didn't. That had once been a long-standing joke, but one that never played well in front of Kate. Though others considered Hap an archetypal bearer of levity, there were times when he was hardly an apostle for jest. Sometimes Hap forgot that when unable to find her Prince Charming, Kate could have settled for a lot of guys, but she instead had settled for him.

At last stripped of his false identity, Hap felt much better being back in his own hide, even knowing he could not dare venture outside. The ubiquity of CCTV and FSB cameras made it virtually impossible to escape facial recognition and probable identification. Being locked up with a woman like Sunny was un-avoidable, but that didn't mean it had to be unpleasant.

Before vacuuming, the cleaners swept the entire place for something beyond dust that might prove more dangerous – bugs and other invasive creatures not of the Creator's creation. Convinced the place was clean, they went about their other weekly cleaning chores. Hap thought they did a good and thorough job, as would be expected of such highly skilled and overpaid technicians masquerading as maids. One of them was equally adept in the kitchen, and prepared Hap a delicious lunch, as it would be another six hours before Sunny got home.

Since he could hardly venture outside, which is what he wanted to do, Hap did what he had been instructed, which was to read the thick file entitled *Bad Bear Down* that had been left on his bed. Alongside the file was a newly encrypted cellphone to replace the one issued at Fort Meade in case it had somehow been compromised along the way. Though basic security hygiene protected against most of the malicious viral infections by hackers, it was now abundantly clear that Sunny Day took no chances.

Once the cleaning crew departed, and like any good spy, Hap couldn't resist exploring every part of Sunny's apartment. Besides, before forming a complete opinion of anyone, it was important to see the place where they live. His thorough inspection included all of her clothing, which bore her unmistakable and familiar scent, and one which he had not forgotten. Though he had no real need to do so beyond prurient curiosity, Hap had no misgivings about going through all her things, knowing she would have expected that of him. Finding certain intimate items on display and arranged just so, he imagined she had likely done this to accommodate his personal inspection and private enjoyment.

He was happy to find that one of the rooms was dedicated to her artwork alone and served as a makeshift studio for her painting. It was obvious she had honed her craft and gotten much better over the years, which Hap attributed to getting more of life under her belt and onto the canvas. Sometimes artists painted a picture of what they wanted the world to see, and other times the canvas was created for themselves only and what they chose to see.

Displayed on an easel and half-finished was one of the latter – a portrait of Hap himself, though the likeness was from decades ago. Clearly, he was meant to see it or Sunny would have hidden it away between many others that were stacked against the walls. The canvas captured the way Hap appeared publicly – impeccably dressed and looking agreeable, but perhaps not accessible. He was equally disappointed that it didn't reflect his affectionate side.

Hap was worried. Taking down the Czar would be the most daring and dangerous operation ever attempted by the CIA, and Hap could ill afford to be distracted or conflicted until it was all over. From the looks of things so far, it appeared that Sunny was doing her best to make sure he was going to be both of those, so he would need to step up his resistance.

# ON THE VERGE

DESPERATE FOR SLEEP to get over the jet lag, Hap had been napping, but was immediately awakened by the sound of a key in the lock. Springing quickly but quietly to his feet, he crept to the top of the staircase for a look. It was Sunny, who had arrived right on schedule at half-past six, lugging what appeared to be a small, but heavy suitcase. Hap watched in silence as she unburdened herself of the full length sable overcoat and matching Cossack-style hat to reveal what was underneath. The sight took his breath away, as she looked every bit as stunning as when he had last laid eyes on her twenty years earlier.

"Okay, Mr. Franklin, it's time, so come out, come out, wherever you are."

"Are you sure it's safe, Ms. Day? After all, I'm unarmed and utterly defenseless."

"Not to worry, Hap, I won't bite, though you know I can."

"Hold on, I'm in my boxers, so give me a minute to get some clothes on and I'll be right down."

"No reason to get dressed for me; I've seen it all before you know."

From the top of the stairs he managed to get another glimpse of her when she wasn't looking. In awe over how remarkable she looked, Hap deliberately chose a better outfit than the one he had arrived in. While dressing, his mind immediately jumped to conclusions he should not have been thinking about, but did so anyway. It had started, and from experience, he knew Sunny Day was an unfailing seductress. He descended the stairs, aware that tough choices were ahead and they would likely be made tonight.

Becoming entangled with her the first time had been a choice, which he immediately knew had been a bad one. This time was different. He was now a grieving widower with only a few loose strings attached. A rekindled fire raged within him as her allure beckoned him forward. It was no different for Sunny. Even years before when first meeting Hap, who was nearly old enough to be her father, she too recognized the inevitability that would define their future. Of course, now that interlude seemed a lifetime ago, and back then she hadn't expected a reunion like this one to take so long.

Beyond that first time at the drive-in when Sunny lost her virginity, there had been only one other time that warranted any memory whatsoever, and that was the mission in Switzerland with Hap. All the other were simply remedial actions meant solely to satisfy her body, but not her brain. Only Hap had reached her in ways no one else could, and this was her long-sought opportunity to make that happen again.

He found her seated in the living room. She arose to greet him, and following a quick embrace and kiss on the cheek, suggested he join her. Her invitation seemed more of a beckoning, and immediately reignited the long dormant chemistry between them.

"Hap, you look great, which proves that men have discovered the secret of aging backwards."

"Bud said you were still ravishing as ever, but I see now he must have been understating the truth. Clearly, there's nothing perishable about you, Sunny. So what's in the suitcase?"

"Just some toys for you that arrived in the diplomatic pouch; you know, stuff you couldn't dare carry across enemy lines."

"May I open it now?"

"Sure, if you must. Actually, I like a man who gets down to business right away."

The bag was stocked with the usual standard tools along with a few others he was anxious to examine. However, unlike the 9mm Baby Glock Hap preferred, the Glock 27 he had been issued was a 40 caliber with a suppressor. Because of the larger payload and snappier recoil, the G-27 required two hands to match the accuracy of a 9mm fired with only one. So despite its delivery of more firepower from the business end of the barrel, in most situations, Hap would rather have the use of a spare hand free for something else. But given all the possible circumstances that might call for its use, he would make do with the more lethal pistol Langley had chosen for him.

"So how's that broken nose of yours, Hap. I never gave up hope that you might at the very least call to give me an update."

"It's never worked right since, except when smelling danger, like now."

"You're in no danger here, but only as long as you stay right here. Your being in Moscow could never be explained as coincidental. And don't forget I'm just another in a long line of undeclared CIA operatives with diplomatic cover."

"Which means the FSB will have far more than a passing interest in your comings and goings."

"Well maybe my goings, as the other only happens alone in the dark these days."

"Given your irresistible magnetism, I doubt if that's the case."

"I've been saving myself till the right guy comes along, and so far he hasn't. Anyway, let's sit for a while and catch up, shall we? But first, after reading the file left on your bed, what do you think of my revisions to your plan for removing Poppa Bear?"

"Frankly, though intriguing, it somehow resembles a made-for-TV movie."

"Perhaps, but one that's been a year in the making. Just so you know, I've put a lot of thought and planning into this, and lobbied hard for Bud's support and your involvement."

"So I owe you?"

"Something like that, especially since you'd already been put out to pasture."

"That's bullshit and you know it. Leaving active duty was *my* decision, not Bud's. For the record, though no longer a hired gun, I'm still a working man and far from retired. At the end of the day, I'm just another guy filling out a time card. The only difference is that I'm no longer on anyone's payroll."

"Regardless, it must have been difficult leaving the legend behind and just walking away into obscurity."

"Not really, but it has helped with the occasional identity confusion and personality disassociation."

"I bet, and also know that getting more about that out of you would take all night, and we've got other things to do."

"Like what?"

"You'll see, but be honest with me – what's your real problem with my plan other than it being mine?"

"I'd rather just put a few rounds through the Czar's heart and head."

"There you go again, still trying to do things the old way in a new and unfamiliar world. Anyway, Sherlock, you should have guessed that the Czar wears ceramic body armor under everything except his pajamas at night."

"Like most of your victims, maybe that's when he's most vulnerable."

"Ha! Like you, huh? Look, Hap, this can't be a shoot 'em up, as there'd be too many casualties and likely all on our side beginning with you. Collateral damage involving our people would be disastrous; if any were taken alive, the truth would be sweated out of them and confirm our complicity. This is serious shit, and there's no room for any of your infamous cowboying."

"You sound like someone else we both know who's also in management, but always far from the battle."

"Bud has my back on this, so let's just do it my way, okay?"

"Well, as I recall, it all worked out fairly well the last time we did it your way."

"You're damn right, so from now on we'll be doing it my way all the time."

"I'm adaptable."

"Like hell; right now you're the loose and leftover piece of this unfinished puzzle."

"What if I *am* the puzzle, and you can't solve it?"

"Then it would be the very first time. Let's change the subject."

"Fine with me."

"I assume you've seen your portrait, but weren't going to bring it up."

"I did, and like all your other works, it's very good."

"And I'm sure the intended message wasn't missed on a master spy like you."

"No, I got it loud and clear, but am not yet ready to go there."

"I've got plenty of time to wait while you do, Hap. Actually, I've been spying on you for years, but you may not have known that."

"If so, you covered your tracks well."

"I had a good teacher."

"I know."

"Knowing I'd never run in the circles where you and Kate moved, it had to be clandestine snooping. I started by watching the two of you at your home soon after Switzerland. You were holding hands walking from the garden, and from what I could observe, even from a distance, was that you were very much in love."

"We were, and maybe more so following what happened in Switzerland."

"And what *was* that Hap? No, don't answer that just yet. The second time was observing you and Dr. Porter at your place on the Eastern Shore, and again, you seemed more than enamored. Then, after reading the file on *Operation Rasputin*, I found out that it was she – your girlfriend Louise, who the Czar swapped for Cherkov."

"Your surveillance looks a lot more like stalking, but you're right so far."

"And disappointed too. Seems whenever I got a hankering to tie you up you were already tied down."

"Sometimes life works that way."

"So what's gonna happen between you and the Doc?"

"I don't know; we're both stuck in our ways and committed to our work and families, so right now we're in an extended pause mode."

"Maybe I could become a distraction."

"You've already become one."

"For now I'm just a walk-on in your life, Hap, but more than willing to be a pinch hitter until your girlfriend comes to her senses. You know, just sharing a little mutual comfort while you're alone and far from home. The reward would be more than proportionate to the risk of discovery."

"Love is a clumsy game, Sunny, but I think I've found it back home."

"If not, I'll always be here for you if that doesn't pan out. I'm only looking for a fighting chance, but enough of that for now. How about extending you a proper Russian welcome with a vodka martini just the way you like them?"

"I was beginning to think you'd never ask."

"Usually I don't bother with that."

"With what?"

"With asking…I just take."

Once Sunny disappeared into the kitchen to make their drinks, Hap could now reflect on the situation and at how fast a pace it had developed. Obviously, Bud had known what he was talking about and must have had a glimmer of what might happen between agents Day and Franklin. The smart thing for Hap to do was to put it aside for now and concentrate on the mission, but given the playful banter, that seemed more and more unlikely. They were inexorably drawn to each other by a host of things that didn't have a chance of being resolved during Hap's visit.

When returning with their martinis, Sunny raised hers in a ceremonial-like toast to Hap, saying, "Welcome, Comrade."

"And to you too, Nikita."

"You'd better get used to calling me Nikki if expecting a proper response."

"Would that be the same as the desired response?"

"If that's what you're looking for. Anyway, it's nice to converse with someone in English only. I've been here long enough that my native tongue has taken a back seat and become a second language after my Russian."

"I'm sure your tongue works well in any language, but maybe you should consider another post before you turn Commie. It'll be a real stretch calling you Nikki while thinking of you as Sunny, but I'll try. You might liven things up a bit by adding a Russian accent."

"Only if it turns you on."

Even from a distance, he could smell the potato vodka on her breath and longed to taste it from her multi-lingual tongue with his. But that would have to wait, as he was after something far sweeter.

"Hap, you must be starving. How about some dinner?"

"So long as it isn't borscht and chicken Kiev."

"Okay, but only if you'll come and help; the kitchen isn't exactly my favorite milieu."

"I'm certain you make up for it elsewhere."

Hap's assistance was mostly limited to finding and opening her best bottle of wine while Sunny went about making a marvelous western-themed meal that included what almost passed as a ribeye. She insisted they eat by candlelight, and afterward got down to business, but not the kind he was expecting.

Sunny was needy, and Hap could sense it. Given her role as station chief and the need to be extremely careful so as not to be compromised in any way, Hap figured she hadn't been with a man in a long time. With Weezie on hiatus for the last few months, he too was overdue for a good romp, and especially one that he expected would be as exceptional as it had been twenty years earlier. Like hard wood after proper aging that assured it would burn longer and provide the hottest embers for extended warmth, Hap wondered if Sunny too had seasoned since that time in the Alps. He also expected that the need for such curiosity and lustful musings would soon be over.

# THE FINISH LINE

CHEATING ON ONE LOVER with another had never been his intention. Hap considered his abiding ardor for Weezie an unspoken commitment, and was all but certain that before things got out of hand with Sunny he could stop it. So far their encounter had been playful, but Sunny Day wasn't the kind of woman any man could refuse. It was equally likely she had never taken no for an answer, and Hap should have remembered that.

He also knew better, or at least should have, that this wasn't going to end well if it went too far. After all, Weezie owned his heart, which wasn't something one dare share. But when called by a different name, anything that might occur with Sunny could be justified as nothing more than a clarion call to nature. After reaching a certain point, the lure of progression to unbridled intimacy became impossible to resist, and this time was no different than the last. He couldn't help but expect this tango would top their previous encounter in the Swiss Alps, and no longer able to control the longing within, Hap answered nature's call.

Since Sunny was finished making all the right overtures, Hap realized it was his turn to respond. She wanted to dance, claiming it was something she missed about being away from home and couldn't dare do openly in Moscow. Kicking off her heels as she moved to the aging stereo console, she pushed all the right buttons, as she was doing with Hap, and an old favorite began to play. It was suitable for a slow dance, and they both knew it well – Elvis Presley's *Can't Help Falling in Love*.

"You shouldn't be at all surprised that I've been preparing for this night, Hap. In fact, I put together an entire sound track and hope you'll find my selections a perfect accompaniment."

"As a wannabe musical scholar, I'm sure I will."

They began to dance, first in a proper sort of way, and then more resembling teenagers embracing at a school dance after the lights were dimmed. Sensing she was now in control, Sunny pulled him close enough to feel his manhood, which confirmed her approach was working. It wasn't long before Hap began kissing the nape of her neck and slowly moving his way along her shoulders. It was precisely what she had fantasized about for so long, and just like that, their fate was decided.

Before the King's crooning was over, Sunny took Hap by the hand and led him to the inner sanctum where no one had yet been invited. As they began disrobing and groping each other, Hap was unprepared for what had been cued-up as the next piece of music. Though it startled him at first, as it would any listener, he knew it was the ideal choice – *O Fortuna* from Carl Orff's *Carmina Burana*. It made perfect sense, as the percussive work was about the inescapable power of fate. Its underlying sexual themes were primeval, the tempo incessantly unyielding, and the pulse rhythmically pounding throughout. It was impossible that such music could fail to excite and inspire, though maybe it would struggle to dominate the sounds they themselves would be making.

While Orff's composition was a powerfully evocative and seductive influence, Hap was convinced that all music was like that and explained why it outranked other powers of persuasion. In essence, music was what feelings might sound like. As such, it had always nourished his soul in positive ways and presumably much like it did for everyone else. Given the ubiquity of music in nearly all of life, Hap was not surprised that Sunny would have a proper playlist for what was ahead. Good music was a universal attraction that stirred what was too often hidden within. Tonight it went far beyond that by awakening and arousing deep-rooted intrinsic instincts and impulses neither of them could dismiss.

What made *O Fortuna* so disturbing for so many was that most listeners couldn't quite grasp its message, let alone how they should respond. Solving that was simple – one did what the music beckoned. Now hopelessly committed to fulfilling the prophecy Sunny had more or less overtly been declaring since his arrival, Hap eagerly complied.

Her breasts were both responsive and sensitive to the touch, so it wasn't unusual that Sunny found herself squirming when Hap's teething became too vigorous. For her it was a welcome combination of both delightful and painful sensations, but she nevertheless cautioned him to be gentle.

"Easy, Hap, I don't want to showcase any evidence of bruising in the morning."

"That'll all be covered up by your bra, so no one beyond us will ever know. Plus, I figured you'd know by now that pain and pleasure are first cousins, if not non-identical twins."

"I do, and you straddle the thin line between the two with considerable expertise."

"Just blind luck, I suppose."

"Yeah right, Hap. More like years of field testing rather than a good guess."

"Well, there's always that to fall back on when in doubt."

"Since you seem well practiced, is there anything else you might be willing to share with this aging broad?"

"Perhaps, but it'll have to wait until I can slowly work my way south into unexplored and unfamiliar territory."

"Unfamiliar my ass. You were there once before, and how I remember, so I suspect you still know the way and can find it in the dark."

"Bloodhounds are like that, and can track day or night."

"Better make a beeline move on it, Hap, and as a heads-up, you may not find me nearly as patient as I have been over the last twenty years waiting for this to happen again."

"I can't imagine where you're going with that, but I'll try not to linger too long, and like the music, will do my best to keep the tempo moving along."

"And why would you do that?"

"To keep you from getting there too soon."

"Too soon? I'm close to being there already."

"Well then, at least not too far ahead of me."

Never intending to keep that promise, Hap took his time by slowly and patiently maneuvering himself down to the source of what he was after. It was obvious that she welcomed his invasion of her most private parts. Almost at once, Sunny's hysteria began to show, evidenced first by her quivering body and soon followed by a cacophony of both whimpering and pleading for more of what she had long wanted.

Hoping to coax him to a new level, Sunny quickly reciprocated his advances with stunning skill and dexterity. Once accomplished, she wriggled herself away from what Hap was doing down below and insisted he lie back and let her drive the bus. Before he could object, she mounted and proceeded to ride him like a rented mule before engaging him in anything more serious.

She relished the precoital appetizer more than he did. Dry humping was something Hap hadn't done since high school and didn't enjoy it any more now than then, but it served its purpose of heightened arousal. Back then it only resulted in soggy underwear, which wasn't the conclusion either of them were seeking this time. So as not to spoil the ending, Sunny made sure it was only a brief teaser of what was to come. Once her joy ride was finished, she was ready for the real deal.

She knew she needed to provide Hap some manual guidance to the intended destination, but in the heat of passion had forgotten that he was better endowed than any others she had shown the way. However, upon grabbing him, she was immediately reminded that it would hurt a little at first, but once inside the pleasure would soon overcome the pain. Because Sunny could only help with the entrance, she was relieved as Hap took his time getting all the way home by slowly and methodically stepping-up the burrowing until she was fully impaled.

Sunny was right, as the initial discomfort was quickly forgotten and replaced by her uncontrollable screams of delight and satisfaction. Coming in waves, her extended rapture was unlike any before and, when nearly delirious, she lost count. She bent over to administer a face-to-face embrace and fevered kiss during what was an extended penetrating finish. For Hap, the ease of final entry and the fury which followed confirmed that this was what he really came for. Moscow and his unfinished business with the Czar could wait.

Convinced that nobody could do it better, Sunny was already thinking about a second and third helping. She was not about to miss any opportunity while Hap remained captive and under her care. Her motivation was understandable. Following their first tasting years ago, she had never again experienced such passion. With the others that followed, she found herself faking it to keep their egos intact, only to finish the job later by herself when all alone and with the occasional help of a hand-held appliance. With Hap, she needed no such substitute, and with any luck, perhaps she could finally stop auditioning any understudies.

Now sated beyond their expectations, but remaining wrapped in one another's arms, neither could speak, as each of them preferred to savor a private reflection on what had just occurred. They dozed in silence for nearly an hour, each lost in separate thoughts about what had happened.

Once fully awake and unable to resist the obligatory second helping, their lovemaking continued apace. After repeating what they had already done so well the first time with Sunny in charge, this time her plan included using a different approach, but headed to the same destination. Eschewing the previous missionary and cowgirl positions for something novel instead, she quickly got on all fours to accept him.

As was fast becoming routine, when it was all over and the panting had slowed, it was clear they both needed a breather. After a short slumber, she was the first to break the silence.

"Hap, this has been wonderful and long overdue."

"Yes, and it was also a long time coming."

"Any girl would be grateful for that. But seriously, somehow I knew it would be as good as it once was, and you didn't disappoint."

"That's good to hear, as I'm no spring chicken like you. Hell, I'm probably older than some of your ancestors."

"Then you'd better take another look because you might not be so inclined when you awaken and see me without makeup in the morning."

"I don't think so, Nikki, and when you arise you'll likely find me in the same state and hard at work again."

"I would hope so, and how I remember. Plus, I have yet to show you my signature approach, which is quite a move."

"It's so like you to hold out on me by holding something back."

"A gal's gotta keep something in reserve for a future surprise. After all, you should never let a lover know that's all you can give. Speaking of hard work, as station chief, I can and probably should be all business, but that can wait till morning. Tonight you're all mine, and having just verified that your undercover skills remain intact, tomorrow we can focus on the mission. But right now you need a good night's sleep, and you've certainly earned it."

# MY WAY

A S WAS HIS DAILY CUSTOM, Hap was up at sunrise the next morning, and finding himself already aroused, got back to work as promised. It didn't take Sunny long to respond in kind. This time there would be one procedural change up from the previous night. As she started to assume her favored topside position of dominance, Hap decided otherwise. Under most circumstances, he would be yearning to go all the way with her in any way she chose to take him, but it was equally important that he exert some of his own mastery to where this was again headed.

In one seamless move, he rolled her over, placed her legs over his shoulders and slid down to start from the bottom. As any woman might, she had a fleeting remembrance of her first teenage pelvic exam. Her legs dangling over Hap's broad shoulders was not much different than being in stirrups, except that her apprehension was of an entirely different kind than when submitting to her doctor. With Hap in charge, she knew what was coming, and she welcomed it.

"I really don't need any coaxing, Hap."

"All women need a little foreplay, Nikki; just ask around."

"Well, I hope you'll soon be working your way up, as I'm thirsting for what comes next and goes bang."

"I'm parched too, and don't forget that the tongue can be a great divining rod for finding moisture."

"Just don't forget what Mary Poppins said."

"Mary Poppins?"

"A job begun is a job half done."

"Then I'd better get back to work."

"But not too fast; I wouldn't want you to launch too far ahead of me."

It wasn't long after he began his exploratory mission that her legs went limp as she beckoned him onward with what sounded like the cooing of a bird summoning its mate. When Hap judged her time was near, he abruptly and prematurely abandoned his work below deck, leaped forward and landed squarely atop Sunny's writhing body as her legs fell from his shoulders to encircle his waist.

At first she only undulated patiently, but once he was inside, she became more like a bucking bronco trying to throw its rider. Of course, she was careful not to dislodge him completely, but just enough to guarantee enhanced penetration as their bodies pounded away. As she should have expected, Hap was equally competitive and held on while boring deeper into her midst with every successive stroke.

Competitive bronc riding was often done bareback as well, and oddly enough, few people knew that the best bucking horses were usually mares. Chosen over stallions for their superior agility and bucking ability, they never failed to go the distance when ridden. It would not be an exaggeration to say that Sunny would be judged a standout had this been a rodeo event.

After going the distance, she cried aloud to signal that the race was over for her, and only then did Hap unleash his own explosive finale to further extend her rapture. Sunny liked surprises, and especially that one, to which she responded with yet another full-body shudder of joy and complete contentment.

Once their hearts resumed a normal pace, it was Hap who spoke first.

"That was some ride, Nikki, and it's clear you're no longer the Sonoma lamb once called Sunny that I first met when fresh from The Farm."

"They didn't teach this at The Farm, Hap, but you always bring out the best in me, whether on or off the job. I suppose you've guessed by now that with you in the saddle, I'm driven to near apoplectic thoughts and actions. Not only can you deliver the payload, but you're unlike any rhinestone cowboy I've ever known."

"I learned to tame horses as a kid on my uncle's farm, but have no intention of breaking you, even if I could. You're way too wild for that, and in just the right and wrong ways."

"You can't fool me, Hap; you were exerting a little of your own brand of dominance there, and maybe to challenge my authority over the mission."

"Sometimes it's hard to refrain from applying a little of my homemade subliminal discipline, and you could use a taste of that special brand from time to time. But yes, you're right, I do have an alternative plan in mind for the Czar, but it'll take a little longer to set up."

"I'll consider any and all suggestions. Plus, having you around for a few extra days might be a good idea after all; if all else fails, you can at least keep my bed warm."

"Maybe so, but Bud may have a hard time buying it."

"Well fuck him; we're gonna do this my way."

"Or mine, Nikki."

"I was wondering when your orneriness and anomalous behavior would show. You *really* can be difficult."

"So I've been told, though difficult may be the wrong word."

"Okay, I'll walk that back, Hap. But you once were, and apparently still are, something of a restless and dangerous tsunami. To me, you remain somewhat of an enigma yet to be fully reckoned with."

"Trust me; you don't have enough time to figure me out if we're gonna get the job done right."

As was often the case, that time he couldn't help himself. Hap liked being in charge and doing things his way; it was how he had gotten where he was in life. At least Bud had known that from the beginning and had given Hap plenty of free rein to improvise. But Sunny hadn't, or if she had, wasn't about to give in without a face-saving compromise.

As for Hap, he figured that "bossing the job", as his father had always insisted upon, was simply one of the afflictions of aging. As such, he had chalked it up to nothing more than getting older and wiser. Plus, he didn't think he was all that different from any others who found themselves in the same boat. Most leaders enjoyed leadership. Hap did too. He was like that, and just couldn't help it because that's the way he was.

"Must it always be *your* way, Hap?"

"If you mean my way or the highway, then pretty much, and following my own path has worked out fairly well so far."

"So I've heard, but you can't upset and reinvent how we do things here in Russia. I've invested a lot of taxpayer dough and human capital setting up the groundwork for this caper long before you arrived."

"But I've been thinking about this for ten years since Kate's murder. You may think you've been around here long enough to know what's what, but maybe you don't know what's right."

"And you do? Penetration of state security measures and infiltrating the Czar's inner circle wasn't easy, and I'm not about to compromise my assets."

"Look, Nikki, it's not like you're burning any resources; all your moles will come in handy during the slow transition to democracy. If they pan out, some of them may find a front row seat when we reshuffle the deck chairs here."

"You seem to forget that over here even the slightest suspicion of espionage is handled swiftly and brutally."

"I'm sure they all knew the risk/reward tradeoff before making the decision to jump ship."

"Nevertheless, I feel obliged to keep my recruits alive for any rewards they're entitled to."

"Dammit, they may have joined the right team, but they're still traitors to their own country."

"The Czar isn't Russia; he's an imperialistic and malevolent megalomaniac from a bygone era. The souls of the Russian people, especially the younger generations are, for the most part, genuinely good, and the rest can be reprogrammed to be better."

"Not until raising all remnants of the iron curtain and eliminating the economic and digital barricades encircling the country."

"Just think, Hap, if we're successful, the global isolation he has created will soon fade away and our real work can begin."

"Seems to me your real work began last night and continued this morning."

"I've never been one to be shy or demure about getting what I want, and that includes you. But now I must get to the Embassy, so how about showering with me before I leave; I'll even scrub your back and other places you can't reach."

"Only if I can return the favor."

"And one more thing, you'll be all alone here until later in the day, so try to behave yourself for a change."

"That'd be new territory."

"Seriously, stay away from the windows and don't open the sound-proof curtains; the FSB has eyes and ears on this place day and night."

Recalling what he had learned at Fort Meade about high tech surveillance and the microscopic bugs hidden within what appeared to be real bugs, Hap knew most of these devices were undetectable. This was one time he couldn't afford to be curious or foolish enough to test the technology by getting anywhere near where he might be spotted or overheard. Snooping behind closed doors and windows was fast becoming routine, but in certain circumstances – like protecting a station chief's home, such invasive techniques had so far been foiled by the wizards at the Fort. Or so Hap hoped, as he didn't want any intercepted video or audio from last night showing up on the screens of either the Russkies or Team USA.

"If you get bored, Hap, and I know you will, you can start getting up to speed by examining what's on the flash drive I left next to your laptop."

"How much material?"

"Two gigabytes, which oughta keep you busy all day."

"I'm sure I can sift through that quickly by ignoring or discarding the unessential chaff."

"I doubt it. Beyond other juicy background nuggets, it's the best intel we have on the Bad Bear's daily routine and when he's exposed. And don't you dare think about attempting a foolish and typical end-run play by improvising my plan."

"Aww Nikki, why take the fun out of it? I suppose there'll be a test on this reading material when you return."

"You bet, so study hard, Hap."

"Will the questions be hard too?"

"Harder than you're used to."

"Well, in that case, maybe you should stay here today and homeschool me."

"You might turn out to be an unruly, petulant child, which, as Churchill once said when accused of ending a sentence with a preposition, is 'something up with which I will not put.'"

"Good, that might beg for even more discipline."

# HOUSE ARREST

H AP DIDN'T LIKE BEING HOUSEBOUND any less than the times when he actually had been held prisoner when undertaking other side jobs for the CIA. He absolutely hated being all locked up, but knew the dangers of discovery and abided Sunny's warnings. FSB enforcement was anything but lackadaisical, especially when on the Motherland's home turf. Having experienced captivity by ruthless Russians and suffering the savagery of Dmitri Cherkov's interrogation in Brussels a few years earlier, Hap knew he wouldn't be as lucky surviving a similar incarceration at Lubyanka, where torture was an art form.

Paging through the sundry documents and analyses on Sunny's flash drive wasn't that revealing, as Hap had done his homework long before setting foot in Russia. What was surprising was the enormity of wealth drained from the country by the Czar and his cronies. The wholesale theft orchestrated by Kremlin insiders had robbed the people of their vitality and remaining threads of hope. With the benefit of preferential treatment during governmental auctions of all industries, there were now hundreds of oligarchs who had stolen hundreds of billions. Apart from their allegiance, all remained tethered to the Czar through ongoing payoffs.

Not surprisingly, most of them now conducted their piracy from afar, preferring to live elsewhere in countries free of controversy and not governed by a tyrannical regime like their homeland. It was no secret that many preferred London, which had become a magnet for immigrants of all stripes and often the most dangerous extremists. Openly living in luxury after purchasing multimillion-pound historical mansions once the sole province of noblemen and lords, the visible splendor of the oligarchs was rivaled only by the royal family. It was no wonder the city was often referred to as Londongrad.

None of the oligarchs' digs could rival the luxuriance of the many palaces that directly or indirectly belonged to the Czar. Their values were estimated to be in the billions. Beyond the mansion on the Black Sea, his favorite was the sprawling lakeside residence in Valdai where his much younger mistress and their secret children lived. A virtual fortress guarded by a military air defense system and a platoon of soldiers at-the-ready for any kind of ground assault, it was accessible by armored train. The more than 80 buildings comprising the 250-acre estate offered every conceivable creature comfort, so it was not surprising that the palatial forested hideaway was where the Czar spent most of his time.

Beyond satellite surveillance photos of the compound, Sunny's thumb drive included an array of bootlegged interior shots taken by a staffer at the compound working undercover. The ostentatious display of unfathomable wealth was evident and far exceeded how the legitimate Tsars had once lived. Each room featured the very best works of the finest European artisans. The photos made Hap cringe, and his indignation was understandable.

What he found even more disturbing was the documented financial complicity of U.S. banks, which for years had turned a blind eye while salivating over the excessive fees charged when washing money for identifiable foreign shell companies owned by the Czar and his oligarchs. Curiously, so far there had been no severe penalties imposed by the Fed or Comptroller of the Currency for such illicit behavior. Hap knew some of the CEOs of these banks personally and had heard their public and private harangues about burdensome overregulation. Surely these champions of self-regulation were aware of the corruption they enabled. Nevertheless, once back home he would make a point of enlightening them if they weren't.

There were a lot of other things Hap would begin doing differently if this mission proved successful and he escaped unscathed. Some he'd move to the top of his bucket list. But right now he was tired of reading the classified dossiers, choosing instead to stretch out on the couch, close his eyes and re-think the variety of roles Sunny had envisioned for him in her plans.

The attributes that made Sunny such a good spy were the same ones that had prevented her from sustaining relationships. She could hook up, but was incapable of partnering up. Of course, her skill in hooking up was precisely what was needed to turn a Russian into a productive asset for Uncle Sam. Given her fluency in the language and enticing persona, most men were rendered nearly helpless, and all eventually succumbed to her wiles. She had a special intuition for spotting weakness in others and a knack for exploiting such flaws until the targeted turncoat heeled to her will. She was cleverly careful never to make recruitment seem like a defection. Instead, her recruits came away from their treasonous actions believing they were doing the right thing and unaware of her underlying guile.

Sunny was more than manipulative, and for most, resisting her wasn't even possible. For Hap, proof of her cunning wasn't hard to come by, as she had now effectively compromised him twice in twenty years. Until meeting her, he had always thought of himself as unassailable, which was a claim he could no longer make. But no matter, for if such a frailty was his only vulnerability, he would learn to live with it.

Just as Hap was about to go bonkers from being cooped up all day, Sunny returned. Sensing he was beleaguered and agitated, she said only, "How was your homework, Hap?"

"Overkilled with background, but clearly absent a definitive mission plan."

"That's because there are several possible options, and since none can be reduced to writing for fear of disclosure, I'll walk you through the various scenarios one at a time."

"What? You have me holed up here for God knows how long without a definitive course of action?"

"Despite our best guesses as to when and where he'll be most vulnerable, the Czar is an elusive target. He routinely changes up his schedule in unpredictable ways and sometimes on a moment's notice to keep everyone around him off balance. That includes members of his own security detail, who are randomly selected every morning for daily duty."

"That's fairly sobering. So we just sit tight and be ready to take advantage of the right opening?"

"Look, like everyone else in the Czar's orbit, we're subject to his lunacy and paranoia. We can only take what opportunity he gives us."

"But Nikki, that'll be on very short notice."

"That's why we've mapped out a half dozen strategies designed around the most likely public places where he'll be accessible."

"And I gotta prepare for all of them?"

"No, the rest of the team has been training for all possibilities, but you don't need to. Bud and I have agreed that would only infuriate you and invite your criticism. It might also serve to distract you, so when we're close, I'll personally brief you with the specifics. None of the plans are terribly complicated, but all will require some spontaneous and creative thinking when put into play, and there's nobody better at that than you."

"How large is my team and when can I meet them?"

"Beyond Chris's techies in California running interference, here on the ground I have about two dozen operatives ready to set the stage and tee it up for you, Hap, but there's no reason for you to ever meet them – either beforehand or afterward. You of all people should know it's better for everyone if no one ever knows who pulled the trigger on this one."

"Oh, so I'll be armed for the kill shot?"

"Maybe, but probably not if presented with the situation we're hoping for. If his people sense any inkling of a weapon you'd be riddled with bullets and dead before hitting the ground."

"That's not the kind of swan song I planned to sing on my way out."

"I didn't think so, Hap, and you should know I promised Bud I'd send you home in one piece but *not* in a body bag."

"Then you'd best keep that promise."

"It'll only happen if you lose some of your swagger and follow orders."

Hap knew she was right, but wasn't about to admit it. Though trying her best not to get caught basking in her newfound dominance, after a leisurely dinner lubricated with copious wine, Sunny put on Stravinsky's *The Rite of Spring* and proceeded to enslave Hap once more in ways he could neither refuse nor resist.

# THE WAITING GAME

THE NEXT DAY IN SECLUSION was not much different, except that Hap was more serious about reviewing the fresh batch of material Sunny had left for him to study. If things went poorly, it wasn't going to be his fault for lack of preparation and mindset. Sure, failure would forever serve to demystify the myth of Benjamin Harrison Franklin at Langley. But far more importantly, it would rob Hap of his obligation to come clean with his children about what drove him to risk everything in pursuit of an appropriate reprisal to avenge their mother's death.

From the briefing material Hap learned that it hadn't taken Christian Franklin long to discover the Russian vulnerabilities Sunny would need to exploit when positioning her assassin close to the target. Given their technical sophistication, Chris's folks had quickly figured out how to disrupt the critical resources that those protecting the Czar had long taken for granted. For Chris, jamming the communication links, including body cams of the Czar's personal security detail, was no more than child's play. Even crippling Moscow's CCTV traffic cams was possible, if only temporarily, so the entire surveillance grid would be down long enough to deal with Poppa Bear.

Chris's work was impressive and hadn't gone unnoticed by Bud and those who were privy to the guarded details of the operation. Though thoroughly apprehensive about his key role in such a dangerous mission, Hap was indeed proud of his son. At the same time he worried that his initial resistance to having Chris follow in his footsteps at the CIA might be on the wane, so Hap's plan was to redouble his resolve to keep that from happening once he returned home. Well aware that any parent's ever-present fear for a child's safety wasn't something that could be dismissed, at the very least Hap was determined to diminish the odds of anything untoward happening to his son. There was so much more that remained unsaid between father and son, and Hap hoped there would yet be a time for that. If he and Chris both succeeded in executing their roles in taking the bear down, there would be.

No less important would be making more or less a full disclosure to Lindsay and Weezie, which he knew would be harder to do. For one, it would be putting the past at rest; for the other, it would bring the future into clearer focus.

Hap was surprised when Sunny arrived home a few hours earlier than usual, but could not have guessed why. Her first words held the answer.

"Hap, it's showtime."

"What's that mean, another rampant romp with your houseguest?"

"Hardly, and there won't be any more of that, as you need to conserve your strength for tomorrow. The timing has been moved up due to the Czar's ever-changing public schedule, so we're now in the countdown phase."

"How much of your advance planning is salvageable?"

"Not much of it, as we're making most of it up on the go due to an unprecedented opportunity that presented itself only today. By the way, Hap, I know you're trigger happy to make a head shot, but you'll never get close enough for accuracy. The Czar is speaking at what will be portrayed as an impromptu public forum, but staged by the state media. It's all part of the PR effort to improve his sagging image by being seen outside the Kremlin walls and connecting with the commoners. Though not distanced from the crowd and behind bullet-proof glass as usual, he'll still be surrounded by a legion of bodyguards that will fan out among the spectators. His private security detail will remain, as always, only a few steps away."

"I think I'm gonna like challenging the Czar's invincibility, especially right here in the cradle of communism. So what's my role, Nikki?"

"You probably know he doesn't shake hands with people who haven't been swabbed for presence of any infectious material. Even in meetings inside the Kremlin with those he should supposedly trust, he sits alone at the far end of a sixty-foot conference table. So since you can't get to *him*, tomorrow he'll be brought to *you*, but on a stretcher."

"Huh?"

"There's always an EMS ambulance nearby whenever he appears in public and you'll be on it."

"Doing what, saving his life after somebody else takes the shot?"

"No, we've arranged for you to be the sole primary responder aboard the ambulance to administer first aid as it races to the nearest hospital, which is about four miles away. The driver will also be one of ours, so you can do what you need to in front of him. The security agents will be in chase cars behind you. Even with sirens and flashers to cut through traffic, the trip will give you about six minutes to finish the job."

"What job and who begins it before I get my hands on him?"

"Let me back up. We'll begin by detonating a small explosive device across the street from where he's speaking that'll set everything in motion. By then Chris will have scrambled all communication by knocking out the cell towers and jamming transmission of any two-way radio signals. This distraction will bring on confusion if not complete chaos. Already on edge and fearing something worse is in the cards, his detail will surround and shield him with their own bodies. Due to plenty of mock training, their common instinct will be to pile on top of him to take any gunfire intending for the Bear. One of them, recruited by me more than a year ago, will inject a tranquilizer into the Czar's head, hands, neck or whatever limb he ends up protecting during the commotion."

"And how does he get away with doing that with so many others close at hand?"

"Surreptitiously, and through a tiny pin dart affixed to his finger and protruding through a gloved hand. When the Czar goes under and his security team finds no apparent wounds, they'll assume it's a heart attack and, relying again on their strict training for such a predicament, will load him into the ambulance per established protocol."

"You'll be all alone with him for the trip to the hospital, but once you arrive and before the real medics take his vitals and determine he's a goner, you need to disappear."

"How?"

"Improvise, Hap, it's your specialty. We'll have a getaway car waiting for you a few blocks away, but you'll be on your own getting there. Since you're unfamiliar with the streets surrounding the hospital, I'm having some video made of the escape route you'll take from the emergency entrance to where your ride will be parked."

"I don't like it – too many moving parts and loose ends."

"But the one part you'll like is that you get to snuff him any way you want. Bud prefers a second and final injection, but all he really wants beyond confirmation of the kill is a DNA match to make certain we got the right guy and not some look-alike stand-in."

"You make it sound like a cake walk."

"For you it should be. Now let me cook you up a fine, farewell dinner."

"In case it ends up being the last supper, does the prisoner get a final request?"

"We'll see."

# TRACKING THE BEAR

I T WAS TIME TO GO TO THE SHOW. Hap never slept well the night before game day, and it showed. Bereft of sleep, the worry and fatigue from the last few months was clearly evident in his wrinkled, tired eyes. But he would prevail, knowing adrenaline alone would see him through. One more day and he could go home, and perhaps with Weezie's help, claw himself back to rationality.

Sunny smuggled Hap and his luggage to the embassy in the trunk of her car. From there a common delivery truck took him to a garage in a seedy part of Moscow where the ambulance was parked and its driver awaiting the directive from Sunny to depart. Once the makeup artist had added further camouflaging to complete his disguise, Hap donned the obligatory white lab coat and draped a stethoscope around his neck the way all doctors do.

It wasn't long until they were off. The destination proved to be a small public park where an overflowing crowd had been assembled for the TV cameras, which was the real object of the exercise. Hap had never before seen the Czar in person, and though unable to translate the Russian's short speech, was nevertheless intrigued by the impassioned delivery.

When the blast went off it all happened quickly and just as planned. After his agents strapped the Czar to the permanent gurney inside the ambulance, Hap worked with the speed and precision of any trained medic. Wearing latex surgical gloves so as not to leave any DNA markers of his own, Hap immediately administered oxygen and began checking pulse and blood pressure levels. Once the patient was deemed secure for the ride, Hap barked his well-rehearsed, but terse command by ordering them all out in a loud and fierce Russian booming voice. They reluctantly obeyed, and once the doors were slammed shut, Hap was finally face to face with his destiny. His real work could begin now that the patient was the paramedic's victim.

Hap had wanted it to be a fair fight that ended with him beating the Czar to death, but that wasn't going to happen. For years he had dreamed that the cause of death would be equally as grim as it had been for Kate. Simply eliminating life from a man who was already incapacitated by drugs didn't seem a proper justice for either of them. But the risk of leaving him poisoned, but still breathing, might allow for a desperate intervention before the lights went out. There was always the chance that Narcan, or some antidote like it, could be dispensed at the last moment. No, beyond making sure there was no longer a beating pulse before making his getaway, Hap wanted the moment of death to be something the Czar would experience with all his senses.

Once the mild tranquilizer quickly wore off and the Czar's hollow, unblinking eyes were wide open, he said nothing while staring intently at Hap. The penetrating eyes said it all, providing unmistakable evidence of the satanic evil that lurked within. Hap returned the blank stare in kind, as if examining the underbelly of the Czar's soul in search of anything redeemable.

The Czar spoke little to no English and Hap no Russian, but that didn't mean the message Hap wanted to convey wouldn't be understood. All he wanted to ensure was that the Czar knew who his assassin was. From that identification alone he would quickly figure the rest out before it was lights out. Though perfect strangers, there was an unspoken understanding between the two men. In many ways, they had been sparring for years, yet neither could have imagined their quarrel might end like this. Hap had come to do what he must to even the score by taking an eye for an eye –

that's how revenge and justice worked in their worlds, and both of them understood that.

Unsure if the Czar would recognize him behind the beard and disguise, Hap made certain by pointing to his own face and said, "Guess what – I'm Hap Franklin, and I've come for you." Suddenly the telltale look of terror filled the Czar's eyes, but he remained mute. Next his entire body stiffened in recoil, which was all Hap needed to confirm the Bear's recognition of his executioner and fear of what was coming next.

A closely guarded secret, but one all the foreign intelligence agencies knew to be fact, was that the Czar both understood and spoke more English than he publicly ever let on. He had spent time at the top secret academy established decades earlier by the KGB to train young sleeper agents before infiltration across most western nations, but particularly America. Dubbed the Charm School, it prepared hundreds of spies to blend into cultures and mindsets that they and their masters planned to destroy.

Though it didn't matter if the Czar comprehended it or not, Hap said aloud what he was thinking anyway. "This is for all the lives you destroyed, but mostly for robbing Kate of everything – not only her life, but enjoying our children and never getting to meet her grandchildren. Taking your life is hardly just compensation, but it'll have to do."

Realizing this was the end of the line and nothing more than justifiable payback for his own misdeeds, instead of pleading for his life, the Russian strongman slowly turned his stone cold stare into the familiar disingenuous smirk he was known for. Clearly, there would be no deathbed confession of his having ordered Kate's murder. Of the thousands he had slain, there had to be a few that stood out, and he assuredly would have remembered ordering the hit on Hap's wife. Though keeping silent preserved his deniability, the Czar's smug smile betrayed him, and effectively confirmed his guilt.

Even if Hap had had the luxury of pausing for another moment of reflection while intensifying the Czar's terror, this was no time for mistaken mercy. After taking a final look for any remnant of repentance, and finding none, he finished the job. Instead of by the lethal injection he had been tasked to administer, Hap wanted the Czar's death to be more personal. After considering several equally excruciating alternatives, he chose strangulation.

Hap had hoped for more of a struggle, but the sedative's effect must have weakened any defensive attempts at self-preservation. Though the Czar's arms and legs flailed in a desperate last-ditch move of retaliation, once his larynx was crushed, he offered little resistance. He tried in vain to gasp, but the choked-off windpipe prevented any trace of air to his hungry lungs.

Unable to stop there, Hap instead turned his attention to the carotid and jugular blood vessels that ran to and from the brain. The surgical gloves afforded him a vise-like grip, but didn't keep Hap from feeling the bulging veins and arteries struggling to nourish the patient's brain. Their eyes remained locked as life slowly slipped away from the complacent wretch Hap had waited so long to extinguish.

When over, Hap had expected to feel something – satisfaction, relief, resolution…anything. Oddly enough, he felt nothing – not even a tinge of remorse for his role in the assassination. His indifference was troubling. Perhaps he had forgotten what it meant to take a life and grown too hardened to killing, because in some ways it had been just another day at the office. Or maybe he had hoped it might have been more like the sadistic torture and near-death beating he himself had endured at the hands of Dmitri Cherkov some years back. Of one thing he was certain – the contagion from that experience was one of the reasons why his own thirst for unbridled brutality remained unable to be quenched. If resistance to such a temptation wasn't possible, Hap feared that he could become his own worst assailant.

As instructed, Hap took a DNA sample from the corpse, but not the one he had been ordered to retrieve. Rather, spurred by the darkest of impulses and with clinical precision, he removed a small body part instead. Awaiting the ambulance's arrival at the hospital was a crowd of medical personnel to whisk the gurney inside. They were surrounded by a swarm of uniformed police and FSB plainclothesmen. The pandemonium was understandable. With all communication links compromised by Chris, it was unclear who was in charge. In America the situation might be called a clusterfuck to make sure such an event was perfectly understood.

Hap was well aware that he had only a few moments before the medics pronounced the Czar DOA. Other men under the same circumstance might spring into irrationality, but not Hap, who kept his cool while looking for a way out. It didn't take long, as once the Czar was hustled into the emergency room, it was easy for Hap to disappear by just walking away from the hysteria. Though moving at a determined clip, his pace bore no outward sign of being either hurried or harried. If Chris had been successful in doing his thing, there would be no surveillance footage of Hap anywhere close to the scene. He removed the latex gloves, turned them inside out, and pocketed them in his scrubs, which would be burned to conceal any DNA evidence that could link him to the Czar's mutilation and demise. After a few blocks he was picked up by a nondescript SUV for the drive back to Cherkov's estate where the crew would be aboard the plane for an immediate departure once their passenger arrived.

# AFTERMATH

INSTEAD OF ENJOYING THE COMFORTS of the rear cabin, this time Hap insisted on sitting in the flight deck's third seat for the journey back to the UK. All of them were anxious, so not much was said until the Dreamliner left Russian airspace, but once beyond the Baltic Sea, they celebrated by downing some exquisite vodka served by a scantily clad Natalya. Given Cherkov's proclivity for carnal peccadillos, there was little doubt that he himself had chosen her outfit.

Nothing could be said to Mac in front of Cherkov's pilot, but eventually there would be an occasion in the future when Hap would break with protocol and share some elements about his adventure in Moscow. He might even enhance the truth by weaving in plenty of fiction so that Mac wouldn't be disappointed with the mundane facts alone.

To ensure there were no leaks about his involvement, Cherkov would probably execute his pilot when he returned to the estate with the plane after being stripped of its stealth capabilities. Though the pilot was expendable, Natalya was not and would likely be spared. Hap had a hunch that she would remain a captive companion in Cherkov's compound for many years to come until outgrowing her usefulness or youth.

Nary a word was leaked about the Russian president's death for several days due to contentious infighting within the Kremlin about how to carry on with no designated leader in the wings. Even the military hierarchy was kept in the dark so the generals couldn't plan their own coup and dump the politicians. This had made it easier for Hap, and a day later Sunny as well, to exit the country long before news of the Czar's mysterious passing was made public. It was portrayed as a heart attack by the state-run media, which went into high gear attempting to whip up widespread support for a national day of grieving. Their efforts were not very successful. Such a ceremonial affair was obligatory for any head of state, but world viewers could plainly see that this one was half-hearted. Only a few felt capable of mourning while most clamored for real, durable change in the wake of the Czar's passing.

For the Russian people, it was a desperation born of generational apathy and poverty. Even the oligarchs, who had once pledged absolute fealty to the Czar, now doubted that the lavish lives they had enjoyed under his sponsorship could continue much longer. Their forecast was spot on, and they did their best to conceal their plunder in faraway places where it couldn't be confiscated.

Oddly enough, the empires of the former Czar's oligarchs blossomed for a time, initially helped along by no longer having to pay exorbitant tributes to their patron. But after the will of the people had spoken in Russia's first-ever legitimate election, the Czar's former inner-circle minions were in deep shit. One by one, all of their businesses collapsed when exposed for what they were – shills for profiteering by pillaging the Motherland's public resources.

It didn't take long for the total upheaval the West had long hoped for to ensue. Typically, it took time before definitive results of any action could be fully assessed. That was true of everything from medical interventions for treatment of disease to regime changes like the one the CIA had just orchestrated. However, to the surprise of many, dismemberment of the Czar's feudal system at the same time rejuvenated the anemic Russian economy the oligarchs had once manipulated and bilked for themselves. It was a perfect, perverse irony that the Western capitalism Russian people had been taught to fear was what would restore their country.

When the Czar's well-hidden wealth was uncovered and publicly revealed, the world demanded that much of it be transferred to Ukraine in payment of long overdue reparations. Even the Russian people and their new leadership agreed. Absent the specter of possible hostilities that could escalate to the kind of war where there would be no survivors to claim victory, the world's sovereign nations could take a breather, but not a break. A much larger threat remained, and America would now be devoting all its efforts to keeping the Chinese at bay in their quest for worldwide domination through economic enslavement.

# RETREAT AND REFLECTION

IMMEDIATELY UPON LANDING IN LONDON, but before deplaning the Dreamliner, Mac and Hap were shrouded in oversized black tunics and ill-fitting hats so as not to be identified when escorted to a remote part of the base that would serve as their private quarters. Given the hasty departure from Moscow, they were surprised to learn that they'd be confined to barracks and more or less quarantined for a few days until the world made sense of what had occurred to the Czar.

It was always about damage control with Langley, which wanted no fingerprints left behind on this job, and it had been Bud who insisted that Hap and Mac be kept on ice until the heat was off. The intention of their seclusion was to avoid fueling further speculation about the CIA's possible involvement. After digesting the news, world leaders could assume what they wanted to believe, but there would be scant evidence to support the expected claims of American participation in overthrowing the Czar.

Once the time for any blowback had passed, Hap and Mac could return, but while under wraps for several days, they at least had the benefit of enjoying each other's company. The confinement turned out to be a welcome respite and afforded Hap an opportunity for much-needed reflection. Sorting things out with Weezie would be difficult, but after securing Bud's begrudging acquiescence, Hap planned to keep his promise by going straight to her once he arrived home. Forgiveness came in a variety of flavors, though most of which Hap was unfamiliar with. Fortunately, Weezie had always been more charitable, because this time around she would need to administer a large dose of absolution.

The fling with Sunny shouldn't have occurred, but it did, and he had only himself to blame. Although poor decisions were driven by a host of reasons, passion typically headed the list of excuses. And passions of the flesh almost always trumped passions of the heart. Hap had reached the age when such passions should have taken a back seat to other pleasures, like nursing a dry martini, devouring a grilled ribeye, playing par golf or, better yet, reading a good book. But opportunities to be with women like Weezie or, in this case, Sunny Day, didn't come along that frequently.

Inextricably bound to each other from the start, Hap's relationship with Weezie had been complex, complicated, and conflicted. While sometimes also confusing, it was nevertheless always joyful. Their shared past included experiencing the innocence of youth, the awakening of desire, the humility of rejection, the pain of separation, and the pleasures of reuniting. The epic journey also had been fraught with apprehension, peril, and trauma triggered by severe penalties of torture and death. To that list Hap had now added anxiety and guilt over fruit that may have been forbidden, but in this case not necessarily prohibited.

Despite the growing precarity of their lifelong liaison, he knew that reconcilement was the next logical step in the progression of what had been an entanglement fated from its beginning. Given the strength and breadth of that backstory, Hap hoped their special connection would once again prove durable under confrontation.

Having grown restless after more than a week in detention, Hap and Mac were relieved to learn that their internment was ending. With little advance warning, they were again cloaked in the same black garbs worn during their arrival, and then hustled aboard one of the Air Force's modified civilian aircraft. Though designated a C-37B, Hap immediately recognized it as the military's variant of a Gulfstream G550. The plane was among the newest in the fleet of VIP aircraft managed by the 89th Airlift Wing housed at Joint Base Andrews, which meant the flight would be fast and the cabin comfortable.

After takeoff and an extended climb out, a flight attendant attired in full dress military uniform emerged from the galley and offered drinks. A far cry from anything found in Natalya's wardrobe, the uniform's intention was to hide, not reveal, what it covered up. She was well-scrubbed, pleasant, and due to her midwestern accent, was no doubt recruited right out of high school fresh from the farm. A military career was her one-way ticket to a life beyond what the nearest small town could ever have offered.

She explained that security protocol on this flight prohibited her from engaging in any conversation with her passengers, so beyond serving drinks and a meal, she would remain alone in the front of the plane. This suited Hap and Mac just fine, as they were engrossed in reading the latest news from the vast assortment of newspapers from around the world.

# SEEKING ABSOLUTION

KNOWING HAP AS SHE DID, Weezie had been expecting him to eventually just show up at her door as opposed to calling beforehand. After seeing the major headlines, she had scoured every printed account of the Russian dictator's death in search of any mention of what she suspected had gone down during Hap's absence. But much like all other things the CIA had a hand in, the real story might not be told for decades, if at all. Her foreboding dread grew as the days passed. Surely Bud Smith would have contacted her if Hap wouldn't be making it home this time. She knew better than to be overly speculative when it came to all things Hap Franklin. Nevertheless, her angst was overwhelming and her frequent nightmares were filled with terror.

It was late; she normally would have been asleep by now, but had an eerie feeling that Hap was close by, and he was. When the doorbell rang, she jumped to her feet and ran for the door. There, standing in the rain, was the one she had been awaiting. They embraced without speaking a word as she wept while hugging him longer and tighter than ever before. Only then did she see the silhouettes of two burly men standing guard at the oversized black SUV parked in the shadow of a large, canopied tree. Now soaked to the bone, it was Weezie who dried her eyes and spoke first.

"Finally, just like *From Russia with Love*. So, I'm guessing you're who – *The Spy Who Loved Me*?"

"And still does, especially if you'll invite me inside long enough to dry off, though I was hoping to stay a little longer."

"And that you shall, my wayward warrior in wet, but shining armor. Incidentally, you look a lot better and younger now that you're cleanshaven."

Hap motioned for the security detail to bring his luggage in from the vehicle, and after pleasantries were exchanged, they departed as quickly and quietly as they had arrived. They would be back for him in the morning as Bud was demanding an immediate personal debriefing.

"I suppose you'd like the usual, Hap."

"If that means a dry vodka martini, yes; if it means something else, then the answer's the same. So you know, I've just gotten off an agency bird from Germany and insisted on being driven straight here."

"I get it; you're thirsty, huh?"

"Well that too, but I wanted to apologize for not being able to call. Given the assignment, all safeguards were in place and I was kept under wraps with no communication permitted. I'm guessing you know where I've been for the last few weeks."

"It's hard to ignore the biggest news story of the decade, which I'm sure you had something to do with. Correction – after foolishly volunteering, you probably insisted on overseeing, if not co-opting, the entire mission."

"You've always had good instincts, Dr. Porter."

"But why do you do the things you do?"

"You know, Weeze, sometimes I feel the Lord keeps putting me in the same situations time and time again just to see if I'm still a dumbass."

"And are you?

"Well, some might say most of the time."

"Like all the times you keep signing up for danger?"

"Danger?"

"C'mon, Hap, you know damn well what I mean – missions that you're probably getting way too long in the tooth to handle on your own."

"Could be I'm not done building out my brand at Langley."

"Now would be the time to promise me you're out of the game, Hap, and before you get your own posthumous star on the wall there."

"As you know, I've never been able to resist a challenge."

"I'd call it something else, like an inability to avoid temptation in all its forms. In fact, I think it's the internal dilemma that turns you on."

"Temptation is like that, Weeze. We all have different pleasure buttons, but I don't know why you have to psychoanalyze all of mine all the time."

"Because it's what I do best."

"Really? I thought that was just part of your mating ritual."

"Ha, and so far you're the first to figure that out."

"And for the record, Weeze, it's not what you do best. I happen to know there are plenty of other things you do that are way ahead of putting a monkey wrench to my psyche."

"And you've been lucky enough to have experienced all of them, Hap. But now tell me everything you can about your trip."

"Not this one. It'd be against the rules."

"Yeah, like you've ever heeded any of those."

"There have been a few instances when I haven't disobeyed them."

"Then make it up, if only to amuse me. After all, everyone knows you're a great teller of tales, some taller than others."

"Believe me, Weeze, I couldn't begin to conjure up anything that would approach the truth of this caper."

"Okay, but as you know, I have a sixth sense about things, and you seem somehow more distant than usual. Did you brighten someone else's day while away?"

"I try to do that every day."

"And you're good at it, but is there anyone else in the picture?"

"There may have been for a while, but not now."

"Can you tell me about it?"

"I could, but I won't – some things are better left unsaid. Anyway, it was part of the assignment."

That, of course, was a tall tale, and she knew it, because the extended silence that followed was excruciatingly uncomfortable for both of them. Instead, she might have said "bullshit" and made him tell her the truth but she couldn't, and probably didn't want to know the details. Choosing her response carefully, and deliberately using as few words as possible, she stared blankly into his eyes, imagining that somewhere behind them was where he stored his heart and soul, and said only "So you've put me in competition for your affection. I didn't think you were capable of that, Hap, especially behind my back."

The awkward lull that followed was more than disquieting. To her credit, and much to his surprising revelation, Weezie's fixed gaze didn't change from one of concern to anything like shock, disappointment or jealousy. Perhaps it was due to the many years of hearing the private and often outrageous confessions of her patients. Clearly, she was shaken, and Hap knew it. He hoped it wasn't the kind of numbing feeling most folks got when trying to shake off their own disbelief…but for Weezie, it was. As such, she had to keep reminding herself that Hap's business was now all about deception, and that he obviously had become a grand master at the game. If it were not so, someone else would have been chosen to sabotage the Russian Federation.

"Hap, I've often thought that you obey the rules only when to your advantage…maybe like now."

When Hap didn't answer, she knew she had him on the ropes, but afraid to push too hard, she resorted to humor.

"I guess I should be happy that Catherine the Great was no longer around to seduce you, unless she goes by a different alias now."

"Well, Weeze, I suppose that's a possibility."

"And that's all I'm going to get from you?"

"For now, yes."

It was clear that Hap was not about to grovel for forgiveness, so after a few moments of pretending to toy with her drink, and like the professional she was, Weezie picked up right where she had left off before Hap dropped the bomb.

"Okay, Hap, if you're done meditating in silence, so am I, at least for now. Let's get back to your *other* primal pleasure button, which for you will always be an obsession with winning. Put plainly, the reward system isn't much different for an obedient dog. Even with a hound like you, the dopamine bump from winning is the same result you get from scratching the undersides of any dog's ears."

"I didn't know it was that simple; maybe you should have started rubbing my ears years ago."

"No, apparently you're like a bad dog whose obedience I can't always count on, but when I'm sure that I can, you'll get your treat. With that Russian psychopath now out of the way, maybe you'll start behaving so treat time might come a lot sooner."

"I'll try my best, but obedience and compliance aren't my strong suits."

"No kidding!"

"But back to fixing me up, I may need a few more sessions to get it all out of my head where the unspeakable things are stored. For the next few weeks I'll have only the Langley shrinks to confess them to. Believe me, it's not the same as being examined on your couch, especially since they already know I can be unbearable company."

"And I don't? Tell the truth – you don't even believe in rehabilitation, which sometimes makes this insufferable for me. You refuse to march to any cadence but your own drumbeat."

"I enjoy the brisk tempo."

"Let's be serious, Hap. For starters, only you know for sure what's going on upstairs in that twisted mind of yours. Unfortunately, in my experience, ongoing emotional disfigurement is usually a fatal flaw for men like you, but it doesn't have to be permanent."

"And let me guess, you can fix it?"

"Maybe, but in your case, there are no promises. Your list of neuroses could fill a textbook, and fixing them may take a much longer discussion with your Maker when the time comes."

"So even with a PhD you can't absolve sins of commission before my inquisition at the pearly gates?"

"Nope, so be prepared, as the Lord will have a lotta questions after reading your intake form."

"My past may be chalk full of iniquities, but I don't think many would qualify as full-fledged sins. Anyway, not to worry, Weeze; my admission plan for Paradise is rather simple – when the roll is called up yonder I'm gonna check to make sure he's not on the gate when I pass."

"And how are you gonna pass through without being on the approved guest list?"

"I'll be on an entirely different list – the one containing the names of those only God could love."

"Don't you know that somebody's gonna be there checking credentials?"

"Oh, you mean Saint Peter. Well, I don't think he'd be an obstacle to entry, but God himself would be much harder to fool."

"No doubt; he's gotta be foolhardy by now and no longer suffers fools."

"I'll have a list of unimpeachable characters who can bear witness to my character."

"Bet that'll be a short list."

"If he's all out of unconditional love and everything else fails, I'll ask for an impromptu audition to join the heavenly choir which, if like all the others here on earth, is probably short on basses and baritones with perfect pitch."

"Only you could be so cavalier in such a moment."

"I do what it takes, Weeze."

"Bingo, and that's always gonna be your biggest problem."

"Oh c'mon, Doc, doing whatever it takes to get it done has always been my personal doctrine. Maybe someday you'll judge me by what I do, and not how I do it."

"I'm not about to further nurture your delusions. You know, you really oughta be put on the endangered species list."

"Then that concludes today's session?"

"I suppose so, and for this round I guess I'll have to settle for nothing beyond a stalemate."

"Let's call it an even draw, Weeze, but at the same time recognizing that such a small concession is a really big step for one who is only used to winning."

"I'd say that's real progress, and maybe you deserve something beyond a dog treat."

"Really, something tasty, as in right now?"

"Maybe we'd better sleep on it first. This is one time when we can't make up by simply making out. Plus, you must be exhausted after such a long flight. You know where the guest room is, right?"

"Not really, but I'll find it. However, what if I get confused in the middle of the night after getting up to pee and instead find my way to you where I'm used to sleeping?"

"That would be unreasonably optimistic and a *very* bad idea, so make sure you follow the breadcrumbs back to your solitary barracks."

"But that spoils the happy ending."

"Oh Hap, there's one thing I have always loved about you."

"Just one?"

"Your unrestrained subtlety is certainly number one, but you're also an indefatigable tease. Now go to bed; I have an early morning."

It had gone better than Hap could have expected or deserved. One thing was certain. Like some of the women in his life, and especially Kate before her, Weezie understood what made him tick. And it was clear that while she may not have been the partner he had planned for, she was probably the one he needed. Weezie had learned how to disarm him in ways he could tolerate, but without extinguishing his carefully crafted persona. Living with a shrink full-time would have its drawbacks, but making their arrangement a more permanent one also had plenty of benefits… so long as she didn't bring her work home with her.

For Weezie, Hap's confession was a shock that she needed time to process before resuming what, so far, had been a very precious but nevertheless open-ended commitment. Before tonight, she had never witnessed the extent of his insensitivity, which would take time to forgive. Maybe they both were growing tired of pivoting back and forth between their separate lives when apart and the special times of their lives when together.

It was a good start, nonetheless. Everything had gone according to plan – not his plan, but *hers*. When Hap awoke at dawn, she was already gone. And not long after fixing himself some coffee, the burly men in black with earpieces arrived to collect him for the ride to Langley.

# POSTMORTEM

THERE WERE TIMES WHEN COMPLETE SECRECY was needed on the CIA campus itself, and given what had just occurred in Moscow, Hap's mere presence at Langley more than qualified as one of those occasions. Not surprisingly, it wasn't that uncommon for the agency's right hand to be completely unaware of the left hand's activities. That was equally so regarding the comings and goings of operatives. Apart from those directly involved in *Bad Bear Down*, due to the sensitivity of the operation, everything would be highly classified. For now, only Bud and the Director would have access to the information or, for that matter, even direct knowledge of the mission itself.

Beyond possible condemnation from some if the truth became known, but more to protect the personal safety of the team from any reprisals, no reference to Hap's visit would appear in the logs. Even the usual security clearances for entry were circumvented. Instead of using the main entrance, where he would assuredly be recognized by someone, the tinted SUV entered the underground parking lot restricted to only a handful of those at the top echelon.

Escorted by the same two security men who had ferried him there, Hap was given sunglasses and a skier's beanie to complete the disguise. The private elevator served only the seventh floor, and once there, the trio made a beeline for a soundproof conference room that was swept daily for bugs. There, in his shirtsleeves with a pot of coffee and fresh ashtray was the man not known by either of his two names, but rather only as the DDO. Hap had suspected for years that the name on his office door and stationary wasn't the same one Bud Smith was known by the outside world once he left the office at the end of the day.

"The prodigal son returns."

"Is that the best you can do, Bud? I was hoping you'd begin with the merit badge award."

"Given the DNA specimen you collected, that'd be mighty generous."

"I retrieved what I thought best, and chose something the Czar could do without in the next life."

"His penis?"

"I knew you'd be surprised when opening the canister. I can almost picture it now."

"Well picture this – after confirming the Czar's identity, I may have the forensics team forward his junk along to our resident taxidermist to stuff and mount as a trophy for your living room."

"You'd better hang on to it for evidence, Bud, but if there isn't going to be any trace of our involvement, there's a way you could always preserve and cherish the memory."

"I give up; what's that?"

"By keeping it hidden in your bottom desk drawer along with that unauthorized bottle of hootch and a photo of me, but hopefully not one taken today when I look and feel like shit."

Actually, Hap was already feeling much better after getting away with his final act of defiance by awarding Bud with the Czar's johnson. He knew the story would get out and make its way through the building, further contributing to the storied lore which followed Hap Franklin. When retold over and over again, this one might well become the defining capstone of his career as a spy.

"You do look a little weary, pallid, and peaked at the same time, Hap, so I'm not surprised a good night's rest under the doctor's care has both worn you out and perked you up."

"Truth be told, you look absolutely terrible and well beyond haggard yourself. And though I hate to disappoint you, even the best of docs can't perform miracles, so let's leave Weezie out of this postmortem just in case you're recording it."

"Nothing's being recorded yet; Comrade Pavlovich will be in soon to handle that part of your interview."

"Peter the Great, huh? I'd rather be waterboarded than spend the day with him."

"Relax – given what the Czar did to his parents, Peter deserves to know and should get to enjoy first-hand how the hit went down. As you'd expect, he'll be painstakingly thorough, but I wanted first crack at you to discuss all the stuff that won't be in the official transcript. And for Christ's sake, remember that I can't redact anything said to him that shouldn't see the light of day, so just stick to the operational details only and not what may or may not have happened while you did your best work under Sunny."

"Understood, and thanks for your heartfelt concern, but you really do look like shit today, Bud."

"Well, it's the same result from any other op we've ever run together, as I can't help but worry until you're finally home in one piece where I can keep an eye on you."

"Aww, see – you do care, and I'd hug you if you went in for that touchy-feely stuff."

"A handshake is all you'll ever get from me, pretty boy. Now let's start at the beginning and don't leave anything out, including your stint as a houseguest of my station chief."

"If that's meant as an insinuation, I haven't the foggiest. Anyway, there's nothing to tell. The bed was comfortable and the Beluga caviar and vodka weren't bad either – sorta like solitary confinement, but at an upscale Airbnb."

"I bet it was, but since you're not going to elaborate, let's move along by returning to what really pisses me off beyond your usual wanton disregard for authority. We've already processed and sequenced the DNA sample you collected, which is a perfect match, but God Almighty, Hap, did you really have to make it his pecker?"

"You should have expected I'd affirm some element of my artistic integrity. My orders were to remove a digit, which I didn't know was limited to a finger or toe. Plus, and for your file notes, I wanted to make sure you knew how small his manhood was."

"So, you're saying that for the Czar, his manhood would be more of an oxymoron?"

"Yeah, but it's not the kind of moron you or any other man ever wants to be."

"And after performing your own brand of field surgery, did you just let him bleed out?"

"You know me better than that. I immediately clamped what remained of his stub so there was no visible trace of bloodletting that the medics would discover before I disappeared. As to how I accomplished his demise, it was a confirmed kill by strangling every ounce of life from him. I decided poison was too good for that motherfucker, so let's call it a gameday decision."

"Okay, I can live with that in spite of your innovative straying from the game plan. But I'm curious, did you make sure the Czar had a little come-to-Jesus moment to get his head straight before the end?"

"I had no interest in witnessing a deathbed conversion, Bud. Besides, I'm pretty sure he knew it was much too late for a meet and greet with the Almighty."

"Yeah, he'd been overdue for that since birth. Given his perpetual look of skepticism, I'm betting he had some early childhood trauma; maybe his old man abused him."

"Truth is, at the end he wore the same defiant, self-centered, shit-eating grin, but didn't say a word – not a fuckin' thing, which made it easy to squeeze the life out of him. After drawing his final breath, the wretchedness remained in his open eyes."

"Did it feel good?"

"Actually no, and not nearly as satisfying as I had hoped for, but maybe that will come later. I was disappointed that he wasn't a more formidable opponent and somewhat surprised that he didn't put up much resistance at the end when time to outen the lights. It happened quickly, so there was no opportunity for his life to end in recrimination. In essence, he was just another nobody."

"Oh he was *somebody*, though certainly a subspecies of humanity, and I'm sure there will be a special kind of hell for him. So what were you thinking when finally coming face to face with the guy who ordered Kate's death?"

"He bore that customary look of contempt. I bet you know what scorn looks like, right Bud?"

"I do, and know it well from seeing the disapproving faces of way too many congressional intelligence subcommittee members."

"That's because they're all weary and rightfully gun-shy of your half-assed attempts at pulling the wool over their eyes and ears."

"Only the old crotchety ones; the newer breeds of idiots are more gullible. But back to the Czar, did that look of his make it any easier for you to do what you had to do?"

"I suppose. At first, it was an odd feeling that we were no more than perfect strangers, but as death overtook him, we slowly became strangers no more. Unlike other hits, I haven't had any nauseating afterthoughts. I guess sometime down the road when reflecting on the kill itself, it may even seem somewhat akin to a reunion of strangers."

"I guarantee ya that it'll be a haunting and enduring memory you'll never be able to dismiss."

"And fortunately a story I'll never be able to share with my grandchildren."

"There is one immediate upshot – at least you can remove vengeance from your long list of addictions."

"You're beginning to make me sound like an emotional cripple. What would you have me replace it with – compassion?"

"We're supposed to learn from our suffering, Hap, and given what you've been through, you deserve to be a genius by now."

"I'm done with suffering and maybe the wiser for it. Besides, aren't we repeatedly reminded in Scripture to love our enemies?"

"I've never fully embraced that as a commandment."

"That's because you only read case files and not the Bible. You probably don't even have one of those for your bedside table, so maybe I'll send you a copy of the King James version for Christmas."

"Isn't that one out of date?"

"Scholars have made some updates and added the obligatory inclusive language to the adaptations that have followed, but the lessons are pretty much intact."

"Good, I'll use the older version without the revisions – you know, the one Jesus used, as I can't abide all that gender neutral crap. It's not much different than the woke movement since the white liberals stole it from the black community."

"You're beyond a hopeless case, Bud, but I'm sure you already know that. We all need religion, especially in this business, and you could use it more than most."

"From one desperate sinner to another."

"Maybe, but the road to redemption for you is gonna be much longer than the route I must follow."

"Why's that?"

"For me, it's only been a little side work, but you've got a lot more kills on your conscience. Though not a duly authorized celebrant, I'd be willing to hear your confession. Much like you, the confessional has been around for a long time, Bud. I think the ceremony began in the 16ᵗʰ century, so it must be working wonders for unburdening troubled souls like yours."

"You're one implacable sumbitch, aren't you, Hap? I'll get to it when I have some free time, which is why I'm retiring once this thing is all wrapped up."

"Finally throwing in the towel, huh? So who's your replacement?"

"My, you do have an unresting curiosity about everything. Worse yet, you don't even try to conceal it. I don't know for sure, but since *you* won't take the job, despite the wishes of the Director and POTUS himself, I wouldn't be surprised if they choose Sunny."

"She'd be good and a hell of a lot easier on the eyes than you."

"Well, in the field she's been enchanting and at times the perfect femme fatale, so I suspect she can manage people up close and black ops from afar too. But if she gets the job, I'm guessing you won't want to continue being her favorite clandestine asset, right?"

"Right. Plus, I'm done fighting the good fight."

"Maybe, or at least until Sunny taps you on the shoulder for a mission you'll find irresistible. Of course, that could only happen if she ends up sitting in my chair. She's a charmer for sure, and because of the extracurricular synergies that have always occurred when you two work together, I'm betting you'll succumb when the time comes. You oughta know by now there's no vaccine for keeping her at bay."

"I've developed a renewed sense of resolve since Moscow."

"I don't question your resistance or stamina, but once bitten and smitten, there's no antidote for a woman like her. Sunny's got a big leg up, and you know it."

"How so?"

"This job involves a lotta negotiation, and don't forget women are born with a natural advantage."

"Okay, Bud, I'll bite, so what's their built-in head start in life?"

"For starters, they control all the pussy."

"And here I thought it was because women outlive men and end up owning all the marital assets."

"That's not even a close second, and by then they're way past the cougar stage and sell-by date. As for Sunny, she's ambitious, well equipped, and knows how to use it."

"Use what?"

"That natural advantage, which she's not afraid to weaponize to her advantage when in combat."

"Enough, Bud! So what's her current status? Even with Cherkov now in charge of leading the orchestra over there, Sunny won't be safe."

"She's already been recalled, and her extraction was always part of the plan. We couldn't afford to gamble on what might happen to her if the Russkies went beyond simply expelling her as a suspected spy."

"Suspected my ass; I'm sure they've known from day one that she's the station chief."

"Probably, but it'll be the usual diplomatic tit for tat, and we'll get rid of some of their agents here in polite retaliation."

"Bud, we've got more important things to talk about before Pavlovich starts the recorded part of this interrogation. Let's begin with your promising me that Christian won't find a permanent home here."

"I don't know – the lad seems to be catching on here in a big way. It's in his veins, just like it is with you and was with your father."

"Not if I can help it."

"Well, you can't, and when I'm gone you'll have no one to petition."

"There's always the Director or the next one up the ladder on the food chain."

"Maybe, and because you'll have a connection to this place forever, I'm sure you'll prove meddlesome enough to the Director if Chris stays aboard."

"That brings me to a second question. I know Bud Smith is your alias, but what's your real name?"

"Why?"

"In case I miss you and want to track your ass down someday."

"Let's pray you never get that lonesome or desperate, especially with Doctor Porter watching over you from now on."

"That's still a work in progress, and I'm not sure either of us wants to seal the deal just yet."

"Then you'd better get back to working on it as she's just what you need in your life. But as far as revealing my real name, that would be an unequivocal *No Way.* I know everything about you, Hap, but you know next to nothing about me and that's the way it's gonna stay."

"What's the big problem? You know I'd never abuse it."

"Our kinship has nothing to do with it. There are others beyond the Russians gunning for me, so I'll be in deep cover and harder to find than a Mafia snitch in witness protection."

"You can't just disappear into the night."

"Why not?"

"Because you're not that inventive. Believe me, Bud, retirement is no way to keep living a life with purpose. Plus, you'll never be able to resist being in the know and in the game. Sooner rather than later your curiosity will get the best of you and you'll be back knocking on the door here."

"Watch me. Unlike you, Hap, I've covered my tracks since joining this circus, and with any luck, there'll be no trace of me left behind."

"What have I left behind?"

"You've already given back by contributing something of yourself. Beyond the everlasting work here, your children and your books will be your legacy. With both you'll be able to reach out and touch the future long after you're gone. Your progeny will carry a piece of you with them, and one day maybe someone other than me will read all your novels."

"Hope so, but they're not novels; if so, they'd be fictional."

"Yeah, I know, but trust me, it's better to keep *that* between us."

"When you finally bone-up on the Bible in retirement, Bud, make sure to read about the 13th apostle before you find yourself lost, lonely, and barefoot on the rocky road to Damascus."

"Who was that? I thought there were only 12 apostles."

"His name *had* been Saul, but following his conversion, he became Paul, and eventually the much revered Saint Paul. If he did it, you can too, so good luck with that."

# RECONCILIATION

THE FULL DEBRIEFING was a torturous examination with no detail overlooked by Peter the Great. Because the ordeal took all day, Hap was offered overnight use of the agency's Georgetown safe house. He almost had forgotten that was also where his car had been garaged since embarking on the extended Russian safari. That big game hunt already seemed a lifetime ago, and he was anxious to resume a simpler life with some semblance of anonymity and normalcy.

After being escorted incognito from his meeting with Pavlovich, one of the agency limos took him directly from the underground garage to the Georgetown brownstone. Once inside, he decided against staying the night. Elegantly appointed, the safe house was typically reserved for foreign dignitaries when in town to trade state secrets, but Hap knew it was bugged and found that creepy. Besides, he knew where he had to be and who he should be with. The time to stake his claim was long overdue, even knowing it would be all uphill from now on. Sure, there were hurdles, but somehow, someway they could work it out. After all, hadn't the pathway for Hap and Louise been foreshadowed from the beginning?

Much like any five-star hotel, the safe house was well stocked with plenty of amenities, and as most other visitors did, this time Hap decided to take a few freebies. He limited the bounty to only those items he deemed absolutely essential for an overnight stay with Weezie. Beyond the salon-grade toiletries and plush bathrobe monogrammed with the State Department emblem, his full take included a bottle each of Boyd & Blair and Grey Goose vodka, a pound of Mahogany (his favorite Caribou dark-roasted coffee), one lemon, two fresh nutmegs, and a grinder. Pilfering government souvenirs was expected, and after taking inventory in the morning, the cleaning crew would routinely replenish whatever had been stolen.

To punctuate his petty theft, Hap deliberately packed up the loot in front of where he knew one of the surveillance cameras was watching, and when finished, turned to face the camera and gave it the finger, saying "put it all on my tab." He knew whoever was watching the direct feed at Langley would make sure the video clip would go viral and further cement Hap's reputation for humored impudence. After loading what little other luggage he had into his own car, he headed straight to Baltimore.

Louise was overjoyed to see him and this time didn't try hiding it. She had wanted him nearly all her life, and wasn't about to lose him over the trespass he had committed and all but confessed to. After greeting him with a full mouth kiss and long hug, she posed the question he was waiting for.

"I hope you're planning to stay over, Mr. Franklin."

"And I was hoping you'd ask, so let me fetch my baggage before you change your mind."

"Okay, but bring it *all* in, because I'm good at dealing with baggage."

"The good *and* the bad?"

"Not a problem, as my typical patients are laden with only bad baggage."

"Then maybe you can unpack mine too, Weeze. Sometimes it looks good from afar, but it's far from good."

"I've known that about you for a long time."

"Really?"

"I've dealt with other uncommonly gifted patients before, and sometimes their talents get in the way of all the good they do."

"In that case, I'll try to be bad from now on."

"That should be easy for you, since it was something that was hard-wired at conception."

"Though it might come as a surprise, now that I'm getting closer to staring mortality in the face, maybe my bad days are over."

"So you can move on to the next phase?"

"What's that, Weeze?"

"Atonement."

"Oh damn, that's the hard part, right?"

"For you, Hap, yes."

"Actually, I already checked with my pastor and there's no study guide for atonement."

"Well, then given your extensive qualifications, maybe you should write a self-help book; just don't make it another of your crusades."

"You know, I can hardly wait to pick this back up, but only after I've unpacked and had a drink to brace myself for more of your therapy."

"Admit it, you'd miss me if I weren't around to badger you."

"Just so your badgering doesn't become shrew-like, or I'll have to borrow some of Shakespeare's unorthodox measures to tame you."

While Hap unloaded his bags, Louise disappeared into the kitchen to cut a lemon rind for what she expected he wanted first – a dry vodka martini after a long day at the office. She knew the drill and he liked that about her.

"Finally, a martini just the way I would have prepared it, Weeze, but making me wait so long is probably a human rights violation on your part."

"Patience has never been one of your virtues."

"That's because patience isn't one of the seven virtues, but let me enlighten you – there's Faith, Hope, Charity, Justice, Fortitude,

Temperance, and Prudence. And by the way, I'm pretty sure I get good marks for all of them."

"Ha! So you *have* done your research, but not as much as I. From a strictly clinical perspective, I'm more familiar with the litany of Deadly Sins, and there are seven of those too – Vanity, Envy, Lechery, Avarice, Wrath, Sloth, and Gluttony. So try those on for size."

"Though I may have allowed myself the occasional indulgence here and there, when measured against the Seven Deadlies, I think you'd agree that I've fared fairly well."

"Like some of my sickest patients, you're a master at fibbing, but at least you do so convincingly."

"Oh good, then it isn't a disability?"

"Oh Lord, give me strength! But enough of that for now, as I'm weary and willing to postpone trying to repair you for a while."

"All right, but the vodka does make for a nice hypnotic accompaniment to your vitriol."

"Hardly vitriolic, Hap – it's just my way of being provocative, which is quite different than yours."

"You have your way and I have mine."

"You'd best quit when given the opportunity, so moving on, how's the world's most famous spy? I bet quite the celebrity by now."

"That's not the way they do things there, and don't forget that I'm no longer a spy."

"Okay, so *former* special agent Franklin, how did it go today?"

"Tedious, but better than expected. I got the feeling this time it was high time to hang up my spurs for good."

"Why?"

"Bud's retiring soon, and apparently there's not much clamor for a guy with my skillset these days. Seems there's even a growing move afoot to begin sub-contracting the kind of work I do, or did."

"What? You mean they can't use an archaic thinker who specializes in arcane matters?"

"Nah, they don't want a sanctimonious relic around who's symbolic of the way we used to operate – you know, successfully. There's already too much public rebuke of what we do coming from the Millennials and Generation Whatevers. Civic malaise in these kids is hard to combat because they don't understand the history that got us here."

"Hap, you may try to act like an old codger, but I know deep down inside you're sympathetic to their beliefs and values."

"But apathetic to their meddling nature. Like most fellow baby boomer curmudgeons, I'm weary of being unfairly maligned for all the ways the world went astray during our watch."

"We did the best we could, and have nothing to apologize for."

"Exactly."

"Putting your self-righteousness away for now, maybe it's time to repurpose yourself as the farmer you've always wanted to be."

"Good idea, Weeze, but only if you'd help with the spring plowing."

"I thought that event was an all-season pastime."

"With you it could be."

"Once again, subdued as always. You'll always be a rascal, and the trouble is – I'm not sure I'll ever figure you out."

"Actually, its easy peasy, Weezie. I'm a classic conservative liberal, and that's all you need to know – end of story."

"And who wrote *that* story, you?"

"You bet, and we writers can get away with being fairly imaginative, though in any others it would be called lying."

"Hap, you may be a huge piece of work, but don't ever forget that you're *my* piece of work."

"Before you resume your work, do you think I can learn to stop being resistant long enough to let you and the Almighty make me over?"

"You can adapt. All God's creatures do. It's not an accessory, but already built in and installed at birth by the original equipment manufacturer himself."

"If you mean honest reflection, I've been down that road before."

"And how was the ride?"

"Bumpy."

"Maybe you haven't heard, Hap, but introspection is hard to deal with."

"Then I'm glad you're equipped and ready to help with that, as it sure beats self-examination."

"It'll be a costly journey for you."

"How much?"

"Plenty, but a hell of a lot more if it doesn't involve your total commitment."

"So that's all you got for me today, Weeze?"

"Not quite. Like most masterpieces, you're still an unfinished work, and I've got a whole lotta work left to do."

"You should know beforehand that I'm like an anvil that has worn out many hammers."

"So you're saying life has already provided all the discomfort you can tolerate?"

"Probably, and try to remember when continuing your work that I'm very fond of finishing touches, especially the tactile ones."

"I bet you are; you always have been."

"In that case, maybe we should begin by opening a nice buttery Chardonnay to get things started."

# THE STORY'S ORIGINS

Look for the first two books in the Hap Franklin series,
available from Amazon and all major booksellers.

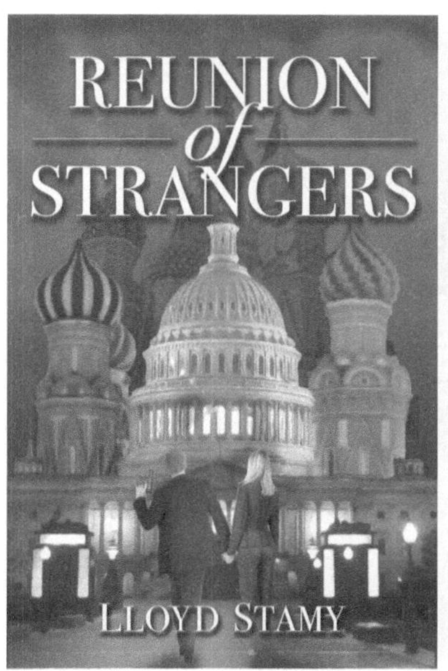

amazon.com/author/lloyd.stamy

www.ingramcontent.com/pod-product-compliance
Lightning Source LLC
Chambersburg PA
CBHW020109310726

48970CB00002B/546